SUMMONER RISING

LAWS OF SUMMONING 1

MELANIE MCFARLANE

Month9Books

SUMMONER RISING by Melanie McFarlane
All rights reserved. Printed in the United States of America by Month9Books, LLC.

Paperback ISBN: 978-1-944816-62-9 ePub ISBN: 978-1-945107-49-8
Mobipocket ISBN: 978-1-945107-41-2

Published by Tantrum Books for Month9Books in Raleigh, NC 27609
Cover design by Deranged Doctor Design

Month9Books

To Tyson, my tovaros.

SUMMONER RISING

CHAPTER ONE

Broken. That's how I feel inside. It's as if something ripped out part of me and won't give it back. It's nothing like the movies. There, it's cold, pale, and filled with sadness and longing, or sometimes very predictable and eye-roll worthy with those Hollywood special effects. But the death I've experienced is more horrifying, filled with personal loss, frequent nightmares, and shadows that haunt the night.

The therapist they assigned me, back in California, said I needed to move forward. *Keep on, keepin' on.* As clichéd as it was, I agreed. I had spent most my life fighting to thrive, practically raising myself. Now wasn't the time to give up. Death was inevitable. If I let the fear of it hold me back, I might as well roll over and die right now. Survival meant I had to push those feelings deep down inside and forget they were there.

"Daciana!"

Great Aunt Katya's voice calls from the hallway while I stand in front of the bathroom mirror playing with concealer to cover the dark circles under my eyes. Sleep doesn't come easy when you're trying to be someone new.

She appears behind me in the mirror, her braided white hair a contrast to my dark locks. "Are you sure you won't change your mind?" Her thick accent is still a novelty to me even though she spent the entire summer trying to convince me that I'd be better off homeschooled like everyone else in our family. I'm not against it—the last thing I want to do is disappoint my great-aunt who flew all the way from Romania to California to drag me out of foster care after my mother's death. After she convinced me to move to a tiny town on the East Coast, with nothing to do but think about my past, I need some distractions in my life. Nothing says normal like public school.

I shake my head and mimic a cheer. "Go Greystone High!" My knotted bracelets slip from my wrist, bumping against the rolled up sleeve of my plaid button-up shirt. I notice my chipped black nail polish that is the opposite of anything bright and cheery. I'm not about to give up my first chance to have a different life.

Katya throws her head back, letting her multi-hooped earrings clink against each other, mingling in the air along with her laugh. She dresses like a bohemian, wearing more bracelets and rings than I thought possible, and flashes excessive cleavage through her flowing blouses. Everything looks handmade, even her clothing, and I'm sure if I ask there's a different story behind each piece. She looks amazing for sixty-five.

She shakes her head at me with a smirk planted across her burgundy painted lips. "Don't be late your first day." She pats my shoulder before leaving. In her reflection, I see a shadow chasing after her along the cracks of the old wooden floor. My heart jumps and I spin around, running to the bathroom door. But when I peek around the corner, Katya is alone as she disappears down the creaky old stairs.

I sigh and return to the bathroom to grab my backpack, glancing in the mirror one last time. My dark brown eyes stare back at me; when will they stop playing tricks on me? This isn't the first shadow I've seen dashing about, but every time I try to chase after them, there's nothing there. I'm obviously out of my mind with grief.

Downstairs, I pop a waffle in the toaster and stare blankly out the French patio doors in the direction of the trees that line the back of our yard. I try to remind my nerves that today will be like every other first day. I'll get myself ready—alone. I'll get to school—alone. And I'll find some dark corner to hide out in—alone. *Dacie Cantar's three tips to new school survival.* I should start a blog.

The pop of the toaster snaps me out of my thoughts.

Outside, my little four-door hatchback sits in the dirt driveway. Katya found it for sale on the side of the road, and bought it for me my first day here on the east coast. Its navy-blue paint is peeling, and there's a bumper sticker that says, *My Kid is a Greystone Grad.* Perfect now that I'm going to be a student there. I've never had my own car before. The freedom is exhilarating.

As I pull up to Greystone High, the stone exterior of the school appears between the thick evergreens. The hard exterior is as old as the rest of this coastal town. On the steps, students gather in smaller groups, each offering each other familiar smiles.

Head down, Dacie. Just get inside.

The school's interior was modern twenty years ago, with classic cement block walls and pastel-colored lockers where more students are gathered. Most of them turn their heads as I walk down the hall, not even hiding their curiosity. As soon as I find my locker, I duck my head inside and finally breathe. I should have known a new location wouldn't change a thing; being different is always crappy, no matter where you go.

"You're new," says a boy from the locker next to mine.

Grabbing my sketchbook from my bag with trembling hands, I take a deep breath. "Sure am." I slam my locker shut, turn, and walk away.

Footsteps run after me. "Hey, I'm Brennan. You must be the girl from California? I heard you moved into the old Marlborough place."

"Hey," I mimic his enthusiasm. "That's pretty personal intel— what are you, my resident stalker?"

His eyes grow wide. "I—uh," Brennan stammers.

A twinge of guilt pokes me in the gut. I should at least be nice to the one person talking to me. "Dacie." I offer, holding out a hand.

He looks confused. "That's your name?"

Slight irritation twinges in my chest. "It's short for Daciana."

A smile jumps across his face exposing small dimples on either side of his mouth as he grips my palm with his and gives it a firm shake. He's somewhat cute with his short brown hair and sparkly blue eyes, which match his jersey with the Greystone High logo. The boy-next-door look has never been my thing. Though I've never actually *dated* anyone before, so I'm not sure even I know what my type would be.

"Why would you move *here?*" he asks, still flashing that all-American smile.

There's a question I'm not ready to answer, and I'm sure Mr. Normal wouldn't know what to say if he heard my backstory. "Sorry, I-uh, have to go. I'm going to be late for Art."

"Come find me at lunch!" Brennan calls out as he backs into a group of girls who start squealing as he stumbles into their arms. I can't help but smile.

I turn toward my classroom, and run smack into someone. My sketchbook falls to the floor, scattering drawings everywhere, while I stand there plastered against the chest of a tall boy.

"Sorry." A deep voice mumbles. I can't help but inhale a scent of pine and wood.

He kneels down to pick up my papers, revealing one of my darker imaginings. *No!* All I need is for this stranger to see just how messed up my mind is. I drop to the floor, grabbing the drawings away from him. In the scramble, one of my bracelets falls off and onto the floor. He picks it up.

"It was my fault," I say, stuffing them back in my book.

We stand up at the same time, only inches apart. We're so close;

I can see his chest move with every breath. I don't think I've ever had this much contact with a boy before.

He gives me a crooked smile. "No harm was done." His voice has a touch of an accent I try to place. What is it? European?

I stare at him for a moment. His hair is a bit long, but it suits him as it falls into his eyes. Those eyes, green with flecks of brown, and yellow like a starburst from his pupil. His jaw line has a slight shade of stubble on top of his tanned skin. He's practically poetic; I finally exhale and can feel my face warm up from thinking about him. He holds my bracelet out to me, rousing me from my thoughts.

"Thanks." I grab the bracelet, diverting all attention from my face.

"Shall we enter class?" Shall? *Who says shall?*

"Yes, please." I raise an eyebrow. The green hues in his eyes flicker for a moment with a hint of amusement. *Is he laughing at me?*

I lower my head and scoot past him, brushing my arm against his. My body tingles at the sensation of his skin. *Enough, Dacie!* I hurry to the first empty desk I see, which is close to the back. Usually, I choose a seat in the front row, but right now, my face is so flushed I need to hide.

The boy follows and takes a seat behind me. I shift in my plastic seat, focusing on the front of the classroom. The hair on the back of my neck rises, as if someone's watching me.

My teacher is an older woman with curls so tight they create the impression of dreadlocks around her freckled face. Her clothes are an odd assembly of ballet flats with gaucho slacks, topped with a frilly apron splattered in paint. She gives us a short lecture then has us begin working on pointillism. I check out some Escher and decide to sketch my hand.

I struggle with making my fingers look correct. They come out more sausage-like than human, which makes me frown. No matter how hard I try, I can't get it right, and I'm not about to reference my Escher print again or I might as well just copy it. Halfway through class, I give up and look around; everyone else is working diligently.

I peek over my shoulder to see what the boy is doing. I should have asked him his name. He's sitting against the back of his chair with his arms crossed, staring at me. I turn back, reaching for my pencil in an attempt to look busy and accidently knock it off my desk. I scramble to grab it before it falls, but it hits the floor and rolls to the back of the class.

I turn my head after the pencil, hanging halfway out of my desk trying to catch it. My fingers brush against the floor as a dark black boot stops the pencil in the middle of the aisle. I follow the boot all the way up to the boy's face. A small smirk lifts the edge of his mouth. Wow, he's fast.

"Thank you." I pull myself up, and quickly fix my hair.

He leans over and grabs the pencil, sweeping his hair from his eyes before offering it back to me. "Anytime."

I get out of my chair and walk over to him. "Are you already done with the project?" He nods. I look down at his drawing. What the—he's drawn a picture of me as I was drawing. Even worse, it's good, really good. My cheeks flash hot with irritation; I'm not sure if it's a result of the invasion of privacy or pure jealousy of his talent. I manage to twist my face from a glower to a frown: "We were supposed to do pointillism."

He folds his arms, still holding my pencil. "I saw something I liked more."

A sharp pain stabs my gut, and my face feels even hotter than it did a second ago. "Whatever," I say, letting him keep my pencil as I hurry to my desk.

Thankfully, he does not attempt to talk to me the rest of class. When the bell rings, he pauses at my desk still holding the drawing in his hand. I grab my things and leave as quickly as I can. I'm not interested in any explanations. Who does he think he is?

My next class is History, where I get a long-winded account of the colonization of Maine starting back in the 1600s. Lucky me, we're going to move through the centuries. After that, it's Math and then finally Lunch.

I throw my books in my locker and head for the cafeteria. I manage to find a sandwich and an apple that look edible, but when I turn to look for a seat, I see Brennan standing up waving at me. I force a smile and wave back, pretending to be normal. Can't be that hard, right? He's sitting with another boy and two girls. The boy smiles at me and the girls just stare.

"Hey everyone, this is Dacie," Brennan says.

I meet Zack, Sophie, and Chantal. Hmmm. Perfectly normal names. They all wear smiles except for Chantal, who stares me down. I'm pretty sure she's interested in Brennan, the way she keeps her eyes glued to him when she's not staring at me, but he seems oblivious as he sits next to her.

"Dacie moved here from California," Brennan says, flashing me another one of his full-face smiles.

Sophie flicks her long blond hair over her shoulder and laughs. "Eww, why would you move here? It's *so* cloudy."

"Long story," I say, taking a bite of my sandwich.

Chantal rolls her eyes. "It's so boring here, but you're too new to know."

I swallow my ham and cheese and shrug. "I've been here all summer."

Brennan's eyes light up. "Really? Where've you been hiding?"

"I just stay inside. Read mostly."

"I've heard about you," Chantal says. She taps her lips with a perfectly manicured nail as a smile plays at the edge of her eyes. "My mom says you're all messed up because of what happened to you back in California."

Sophie shoots her a dirty look. "Shhh." Chantal narrows her eyes and gives her a look.

My heart starts to palpitate erratically, but I know how to hide it. I raise an eyebrow. "What do you mean?"

"Wait," Zack says, still chomping on his sub sandwich. "I thought it was her mom?"

"Shut up, Zack." Sophie's cheeks turn red as she hits his arm. "I'm sorry, Dacie." And it's true, she genuinely looks the part. "We heard, you know, about your mom."

I force down my next swallow. "So everyone knows?"

"It is a small town," Chantal says, leaning forward. I can see it—the hunger for gossip. She's daring me to cough up the gory details of my past. But not today. Sorry, honey. You're not worthy. I scowl back, biting down on the inside of my cheek until I can taste the metallic tang of blood.

"Hold on. everyone." Brennan raises his hands. "All I meant was, we didn't know you've been here all summer. It probably sucked being stuck in that stuffy old house. I would have come by to meet you." He flashes me his prep-boy smile.

Right. Come meet the freak. I put my half-eaten sandwich down on my tray and stand up. My chair scrapes against the floor, echoing in the quiet cafeteria. Was everyone around us trying to listen in on our conversation?

"Don't go," Brennan says. The rest of the table looks away, except for Chantal.

"Sorry." She tilts her head and smiles.

"It's fine. I just need some air."

I take my tray and deposit it near the exit as I leave the cafeteria. As I go to push the doors open, a black streak flies out of the corner of my eye. Ironic, the only familiar things here are the shadows that taunt me.

The double doors to the cafeteria bang closed behind me as my frustration builds. I walk to a quiet corner in the hallway, and lean my back against the wall as I exhale. I hadn't realized I was holding my breath, again. Some girls giggle as they pass by. This normal thing sucks.

I close my eyes and think about my mom. Six months wasn't long enough to stop me from hearing her screams, let alone numb the pain of her loss. The mention of her, and the fact everyone knows the story of how she died, stings like it did when I left the West Coast. Now I want nothing more than to go back there. What's the point of being here if I can't escape the past?

"You all right?" a familiar, accented voice says from next to me.

I startle, opening my eyes, and see the boy from Art. "I'm fine."

I push myself from the wall, leaving him behind as I continue down the hallway to the doors outside. As I reach the exit, I turn and see the boy staring at me. My body shivers from the cool fall air.

When the bell rings, I go back inside, making a beeline for my locker. A slip of white paper hangs halfway out of it. I pull it out and right away recognize it: it's the picture of me from Art, but the boy who drew it is gone.

I stomp through the hallway, determined to find him, but he's nowhere to be seen. Brennan sees me and is about to wave, but he lowers his hand when I shoot him a glare. I ignore him and continue down the hallway. The second bell rings for classes, and the hallway empties. There's no way I'm going back to a classroom with these people today. I crumple up the paper and throw it in my backpack. Again, I catch a black streak in the corner of my eye. I really need to get more sleep.

CHAPTER TWO

When I get home, the house is not as quiet as I hoped. Katya bangs around in her studio, doing god knows what in there. She tells me she's an artist, but I've yet to see her sell anything. Maybe she means in the creative sense alone. Her gardener, Constantine, nods to me as he walks out the front door.

Katya's house is old and what I'd call a mansion, like the ones I used to see along the Californian coast. My only personal comparisons are the stuffy little apartments where Mom and I lived. This house is apparently a Classic Victorian style, and my great aunt has proudly kept it up all these years with the help of her gardener/handyman Constantine, an elegant older man who barely speaks a word of English.

I lean against the door to her studio, which sits off the kitchen at the back of the house. "You're back early," Katya says, looking up from behind a canvas, paint smudged on her cheek just under her sharp blue eyes.

"Bad day. I'm going up to my room."

I stomp up the stairs, and throw my backpack on my bed. Katya appears at my door. For an older woman, she sure is sprightly.

"What's the matter, my Daciana?" I wince. My mother never once called me Daciana. Now the sound of it is all I need to bring me to the edge of tears, even though I know it would disappoint my mother. Mom always said, Cantar women don't cry.

"Everyone knows." With only two short words, she knows exactly what I mean.

Katya rushes into the room, and embraces me. "Oh, my dear." She runs her hand down my long dark hair, and I relax in her arms. Mom never did anything like this for me, but that doesn't mean I don't miss her. I thought I could leave all my sadness behind in California, but it and my overactive imagination have followed me here. I let go of Katya, and embrace a pillow in her place. "Why me?"

"It's a small town; rumors spread fast," she says. "But tell me. Are you still having the nightmare?"

My body tenses at the mention of it—this black mark left on my life. When Katya first came, the nightmare happened all the time, sometimes even when I was awake. After we moved, it happened less and less. But the memory was always there, simmering under the surface of my thoughts. No, I'll never forget that night last spring.

I'm asleep in my bed when I hear our apartment door kicked in.

The voices of two men call out for my mother. Instead of cowering in my room, I shoot out of bed and run into her room. She's already at the door, and hides me under her bed.

I cower underneath there, my eyes glued to her face as she holds a finger to her lips to tell me to be quiet. That's when they kick in her bedroom door. I can't see them, cloaked in the darkness of the night. They don't see me hidden in the shadows, covering my ears to block out my mother's screams.

The tears threaten to fall again, and I know my pillow would conceal them. But I would always know I gave in to my emotions, and that's just not allowed. You don't survive by giving in. I'm a fighter.

Katya runs her hand along my black strands, as if to give me strength in some sort of Samson metaphor. She is a Cantar woman, too. "I'm glad you didn't cut your beautiful hair," she says, as if reading my mind.

Back in California, Katya walked in on me with a pair of scissors poised along my long locks. I felt like I needed a change to make things better. That's when she convinced me to come to the east coast—well first to put down the scissors. Who was I kidding? Nothing could have made things better. Especially not a butchered new hairdo.

"Tea?"

"Sure."

I join her in the drawing room, and contemplate while Katya puts on the kettle. These small moments make me feel normal. Katya's answer to most things is tea. It's a staple to her daily routines.

Tired? Have tea. Overworked? Tea. Troubled? Tea. My favorite part of the entire process is that she likes to read the leaves after we've finished, but I pretend not to pay much mind to her when she does. It's another thing my mother hated from her youth. She told me her mother was a Gypsy. She read palms and told fortunes. My mother despised her family for her jagged childhood. I wonder if she realized how close the apple fell when it came to me.

After we finish a quiet cup of tea, Katya reaches out to me. "Let me see your cup." When I hand it over, her fingers brush against mine, and I shock her. She reels back in pain, and I'm left holding the teacup in shock.

"I'm sorry!" I've never seen my great-aunt look so taken aback.

"Never mind." She reaches toward me, more determined but cautious. When she touches my hand, nothing happens. She looks at me for a moment, then leans over the cup, looking down at my leaves.

"No need to discuss your past," she begins. "We know enough. Always a broken anchor there. Hmmm, what do I see in your present? A bridge. Very interesting. We have not seen that before. It has a sun nearby. Nice, new beginnings. But where does it lead to?"

My mind wanders off as I notice one of the black streaks zip past out the corner of my eye. I turn toward the window to look for it, but it's already gone. There's nothing there but the window and a sunny day on the other side of it.

I startle at Katya's voice. "Heavens!"

My curiosity is piqued. She's never been overly excited about what she's seen. "What do you see?"

"There is a rose in a vase," Katya says. "Very strange indeed. A romance and a secret? Hmmm. I see a fire as well, but it looks closer to the octopus—"

Seriously, an octopus? "Okay, Auntie." I smile. "That's enough for today."

Her eyes widen with excitement, and meet mine. "Don't you see? Romance is coming."

Romance—ha! I wave my hand dismissively. "I'm not interested."

Katya's eyebrows scrunch together. "If only your mother had taught you more about love."

My stomach lurches. I'm pretty sure Katya doesn't want to hear about my mother's preference for one night romances. Nothing enticed me to think about romance less than to see her continuous stream of early morning walkouts.

"I got the birds and the bees talk, thanks."

My great-aunt puts the cup down, stands, and throws her hands in the air as she speaks loud and actively in Romanian. I smile at her unraveling, but then catch another black streak out of the corner of my eye. I follow this one, half expecting it to dissipate in the sunlight from the window, but this time it zips through the glass, across the street, toward the boy from Art, who's standing there, watching me.

I jump out of my chair. "Hey!"

Katya has already left the room—most likely back in her studio pondering the tea leaves. I run to my bag and grab the drawing out of my backpack, before I swing the door open. He's already half a block away. I run out into the street chasing after him.

"Hey!" I yell again. "Stop!"

The boy turns and stares at me with that same amused look on his face. I thrust the picture at him.

"Take this back."

"No." He looks down at me. "It's yours."

I shove it against his chest. "I don't want it." He's surprisingly solid for his lean frame.

He shrugs. "Then throw it out." His arms stay still in his pockets.

I don't know what to do. I've never met someone who frustrated me this way. "What are you doing out here? Stalking me?"

His smirk disappears as he shifts his weight. "No."

Good, I've unsettled him. I toss the drawing on the ground between us. "Happy now?"

A frown crosses his face as he stares at the drawing on the ground. "Not really."

I realize how childish I'm acting and I lean down and pick it up. "I don't want to litter," I mutter.

We stand there, both staring at anything but each other. I break the tension and turn to leave, but he reaches toward me and grabs the opposite corner of the drawing. I stand still, watching him as we hold the paper together and he stares at it intensely. He lets go and looks disappointed.

"What was that all about?"

He frowns. "Nothing." I catch another black streak out the corner of my eye and turn to look; this time he looks too, then glances back at me.

"What were you looking at?" I ask cautiously. I can tell he's hiding something. My mind flickers back to the tea leaves.

"Nothing," he says. "What were you looking at?"

We stare at each other in silence. I want to leave, but I can't seem to tear myself away from him. Electricity hangs in the air between us. It's a mix of frustration and longing.

"I'm Tryan," he says, holding his hand out.

I stare at his hand, then look back up at him. He looks amused at me again, but this just irritates me more. I reach out and grab his hand. "I'm Dacie—ow!" A shock runs between our palms. His eyes grow as wide as mine feel as I withdraw my hand. I've managed to shock two people in the last twenty minutes.

He stands silently, staring at me with something close to awe. Or maybe it's trepidation. Yeah, most likely the latter. This is too weird.

"I'm going to go. No more stalking me, okay?"

I don't wait for his answer. I walk away with the sensation of his gaze bearing into my back. It sends shivers down my spine. The electric kind.

CHAPTER THREE

I pause at the doorway of Katya's studio to watch her paint. She's a flurry of creativity as she passionately sweeps her arm along the canvas, leaving only minute brushstrokes in its wake.

She pauses with one arm mid-air and asks, "Did you ever see your mother paint?"

How does she know I'm standing behind her?

My mother? Paint? I scoff. "Unless you mean her face before going out at night, that woman never lifted a brush."

Katya sighs. "Oh, she did, ever since she was old enough to hold a brush. I have yet to see the likes of her attention to detail."

"You must be mistaken—"

Katya turns toward me. Her eyes are narrowed and fiery as her finger hangs in the air. "I am never mistaken. Do not forget that, Daciana."

Her change in demeanor frightens me. But she soon lowers her arm. "Come in here, please."

I maneuver around fallen canvases and drapes of fabric strewn across the floor. "What is it?" I ask.

"Look at this painting," she says, studying my face. "Tell me, what do you see?"

I stare at the oil painting in front of me. "There's a tree," I say, looking back at her. She nods for me to continue. "The tree is on fire."

"What else?" she prods.

I'm confused. The tree takes up the entire painting. There isn't a single leaf left; the flames consume everything else. "I don't understand."

"Look deeper, Daciana. Really focus."

I take a deep breath and stare hard at the painting. Nothing happens. The ridges of the oil paint rise at the edges of the brush strokes, making the flames lift from the canvas. I stare harder, focusing on the flames, noticing the multi-colored detail in each one, how the flow of colors in each flicker is different from the next. For a second I notice part of the painting move. No, it's just a trick of my eyes. I'm straining too much. Then the doorbell chimes.

"So close," Katya curses under her breath.

I leave the studio, relieved to have a break from Katya's strange test, and open the front door. Brennan's cheeks shift as he smiles at me and I pause before saying hello. He's fit, that's apparent. I wonder if he has a six-pack. I blush at the thought and Brennan takes it as a compliment. "Hey there," Brennan says, giving his full teeth smile, charm and all.

I must look like a silly girl, checking him out in the doorway. "Hi." I start laughing at myself and Brennan beams wider. He must think I'm happy to see him.

"We're going downtown to eat. Want to come?" I look past Brennan and see Sophie, Zack, and Chantal piled into a small pickup out front. Chantal is the only one who doesn't wave.

"I'm not really hungry."

"She'd love to go," Katya says behind me. "It's good to get out, Daciana. Go, clear your head."

Brennan smiles again. "Great." I reluctantly grab a sweater and some money and head out the door. I go to jump in the back of the truck with the others, seeing Chantal in the passenger seat. "Come on!" Brennan says. "There's room beside me." I half-heartedly climb in between Chantal and Brennan. How uncomfortable.

"So," Brennan says. "It's Daciana, is it?"

"No," I say. "It's Dacie. Only my great-aunt calls me that."

Brennan parks at a convenience store near the bay. Everyone jumps out of the back of the truck and Chantal holds the door open for me. Brennan is waiting for me on the other side, but the look on Chantal's face says she's the safer choice. I'd rather not make an enemy my first day making friends.

Inside, everyone's getting drinks. I opt for a slushie. It's been forever since I got one. Suddenly, I miss the West Coast. I rarely get homesick since we moved so much. I guess it's really Mom I'm missing.

"I thought we were getting something to eat?" I ask.

"Catch." Zack tosses me a bag of jerky. "Or are you a carb kinda girl?"

I scrunch my nose at the shriveled up meat. "I was raised on convenience stores, but you still couldn't pay me to eat this stuff."

"Oh?" Chantal pipes up. I ignore her and go to the register.

Brennan leans on the counter next to me so close that our arms are touching. "The restaurant was just a lie to get your aunt to let you out." There's that smile again.

I hold up my slushie. "Kind of figured." I pay the clerk and slip away from Brennan's stare, but that doesn't deter him.

He slides up next to me. "You won't get in trouble, will you?"

I shake my head. "I don't need Katya's permission to do things."

"Noted." Brennan winks. He opens his jacket and flashes a bottle of whiskey at me.

Sophie runs up and grabs my arm, pulling me away from Brennan. "We're going down to the vendors on the beach. You'll love it. It might remind you of home."

Chantal laughs louder than she should. "I doubt Little Miss California will agree."

The beach is behind the convenience store. Seagulls cover the shoreline, waiting for any morsel they can sneak from the nearby vendors that line the beach. A cool fall breeze catches my face as it bounces off the ocean.

"Don't mind Chantal," Sophie says. "She's had a crush on Brennan since kindergarten when he shared his crayons with her."

"What's her problem with me then?" I ask.

"You know." Sophie smiles. "Because Brennan likes you."

"I'm not looking for a boyfriend," I say.

"Who mentioned *boyfriend*?" Sophie smiles again.

Brennan slides in between Sophie and me. "Here." He passes Sophie the bottle. She stops and pours some into her cup, then hands the bottle to me.

"No thanks," I say. My mom drank enough while I was growing up. The appeal was lost on me.

"Oh, come on." She grabs my cup and pours in some of the unknown substance.

I grab my cup back and see my slushie melting under the booze. "That's enough."

Sophie shrugs. "Suit yourself." She runs back to Zack and passes him the bottle, leaving Brennan and me alone.

I hold my cup up to Brennan. "Is this what you guys do for fun around here?"

"What else are you going to do in a small town?" he asks. He walks awfully close to me, his shoulder brushing against mine every other step. A feeling of claustrophobia crawls across my skin.

Zack runs up behind us and takes Brennan in a headlock. "Let's grab a hotdog at the arcade." He turns to me and winks. "Or do you not eat those either?"

I hold up my hands in the air. "Isn't it a food group?" Zack laughs aloud.

I sit near the open windows of the arcade with Sophie and

Chantal, while the boys play video games. I'd rather be playing one myself, but Chantal made it clear I was to hang out with them. Looking out at the water, I welcome the breeze as a distraction.

"Where's your dad?" Chantal asks unexpectedly.

I turn my attention to her. It's clear she hates me. I want to reach across the table and slap her, but instead I plaster a smile on my face. Sophie clears her throat. "Why would you ask that?"

Chantal throws Sophie a dirty look. "What? We know what happened to her mom. That's why she's here living with her aunt. I'm just trying to get to know her."

The table falls quiet again. I take a sip of my drink, forgetting about the alcohol in it. I cough as soon as it bites the back of my throat. Whisky. Great.

Chantal mumbles, "Listen, I just meant we don't know much about you. Where did you grow up?"

I run my hands along my pant legs. I wish I could join them under the table and hide. "We moved around a lot."

"What did your mom do for work?" she asks.

I've dreaded answering this question my entire life, so I came up with a paper cutter answer for people like this; all part of acting normal. "She was a secretary."

"Oh." Chantal looks disappointed. I take another swig of my drink. This time the whiskey burns a little less.

"What sort of a name is Dacie anyways?

"Oh, *gawd*, Chantal." Sophie rolls her big blue eyes. "Enough already. I'm going to go hang out with the boys if you keep this up."

Chantal folds her hands across her chest, pouting.

Sophie turns to me with her lipstick smile. "I took a class with your aunt this summer. I wish she'd told me about you—we could have hung out."

"My great-aunt teaches?" She left the house a lot, but I spent most the time up in my bedroom reading books from Katya's library or surfing the Internet. That was the thing about moving around a lot; I didn't get to meet many people or take much with me from place to place—but books and the Internet were always available.

Chantal's face jerks away from the window, suddenly interested in our conversation again. "Don't you know about your own aunt?" Her voice drips with her usual drama.

Sophie shuts her up with a look.

"Know what?" I ask, taking another sip.

"Nothing," Sophie says. "She teaches art at the community center."

"And she's bat shit crazy."

"I said, shut up, Chantal."

"As if she doesn't know, Sophie," Chantal shoots Sophie an angry look. "She's a witch or something. Makes potions, reads fortunes. Every winter she left and every summer she returned, running up and down the streets warning everyone about ghosts, or something."

"She's a Gypsy. Not a witch."

Chantal snorts and everyone else goes silent. I take another sip, but this time my stomach lurches; I shouldn't have been drinking, especially on an empty stomach. I stand up and feel a little lightheaded. "I need to go to the bathroom," I mumble, leaving the table.

I bolt the door behind me as soon as I get inside. Tears form in the corners of my eyes, but I quickly wipe them away before they can fall. I look around at the tiny room; there's no way to escape. I should've ran out of the arcade and walked home, because now I have to face them all again when I leave; worst of all, see their pity.

I walk over and place my hands on the sink. "You're not going to cry, you're not going to cry," I repeat watching myself in the mirror like some outsider. Something moves behind me, and I spin around. I thought I was alone.

The two stalls behind me are empty. There's nothing else in the room except me, a hand dryer, and a crappy painting of some irises. I think the artist was trying to mimic Van Gogh, but obviously lacked talent. I guess that's why they're hanging in a bathroom and not a museum somewhere.

I run my finger across the painting's surface. It's actually painted and not just a print. Surprising. The flowers by my finger begin to move. I step back. Nothing happens. Great. Now I'm going to start seeing paintings move; maybe I'm losing my mind after all. I start to turn away but suddenly, between the stems, a small grotesque face pops out of the painting.

I almost trip on my feet as I step backward. The creature leans forward, his head like some wild three-dimensional trick, with its long nose leading the way as its large ears follow suit. It eyes me up before looking around the room. "Are you the one who let me out?" the creature squeaks.

I can hardly open my mouth to answer, let alone form words.

It pulls the rest of its body out of the painting with two hairy claws, and jumps to the bathroom floor. The painting hangs skewed on the wall, and the flowers look undisturbed.

The creature leans toward me, as if he's sniffing my pant leg, forcing me to step back against the cold bathroom wall. "So, what are the rules?" it asks. "Back by midnight? Don't steal any little children?"

Adrenaline crawls across my skin. "What are you?" My voice rushes out.

"An imp." It scuttles toward the bathroom stalls and pokes its head under each. "Are you sure you're the only one here?"

I nod my head.

It shoots me a mischievous grin. "Well then, it's my lucky day. Catch you later!" The creature climbs up the wall next to the painting, and disappears between the bars on the window. I turn, unbolt the door, and step out into the arcade. Sophie waves me over, but I can't even manage a smile in her direction. Did they slip something else into my drink?

Brennan steps in front of me. "Sophie told me Chantal was bugging you. Are you okay?"

I move past Brennan, toward the exit. "No, I am definitely not okay. I'm going home."

"Hey, Dacie, wait up." Brennan chases after me and puts his arm in front of the door. "Don't go. I want you to stay."

Pushing him out of the way, I walk out into the crisp autumn air.

CHAPTER FOUR

The ocean breeze follows me home, sneaking into my sweater and sending shivers through my body, but it's the last thing I'm worried about right now. I need to clear my thoughts and wrap my head around what just happened. That creature in the bathroom acted as if I should know it. What *the hell* is going on here?

Even worse, the alcohol continues to play tricks on my eyes—shadows are slinking about everywhere, playing in the trees that line the road as I make my way home. I pull my collar up high and hide as much of my face as I can inside. I wish I were home where I could hide.

Half an hour later, I'm walking up the broken sidewalk to our old house at the end of the street. The lights give me comfort in the knowledge my sanctuary is close. Constantine is still outside, trimming the hedges this time. He nods as I walk past, but I don't meet his eyes. Instead I duck inside, and run straight to my bedroom.

"Daciana?" Katya calls out. "Is that you?"

I close my bedroom door and throw myself on my bed. How am I supposed to tell anyone what I saw? They'll think I had a breakdown, after what happened to my mom. Who knows, maybe I am?

"Daciana?" Katya says from the other side of my door.

"Go away." My pillow muffles my voice. I could speak louder, but I know Katya does not understand boundaries. That's something Mom and I had established well.

"What's wrong?" She opens my door. At least she hangs back.

"It's nothing," My face is still down on my pillow.

"I can tell you're lying," she says. Her footsteps creak along my floorboards as she crosses the room. "Why are you back so soon?"

I spout it out before I can consider the ramifications. "Did you use to run around town, telling people you saw ghosts?"

"You heard about that, did you?" Still, she doesn't hesitate, sitting next to me on my bed.

"Well, were you?" I lift my head, wanting to see her reaction.

"No," she says, "it wasn't like that."

"That's what people say."

"I don't care what people say," Katya looks me in the eye. Her gaze is like ice, void of any humor. "Simple-minded people gossip when they don't understand things."

"I hate it here," I say. It's the truth.

"Give it time," she says. "This is where we're meant to be for now."

"Where are we supposed to go next?" I never wondered until

now if we were going to move around a lot as Mom and I did. Will anywhere feel like home?

"We wait and see where we're meant to be," Katya says. "Right now all signs point to Maine."

"Argh," I say, grabbing my pillow and holding it over my face. "You and Mom are the same in many ways. She was vague all the time. It would be nice just to know where my life is going."

"Come with me." Katya stands, and my bed moves in unison. "Let's go to the studio again."

I reluctantly follow her down the staircase, running my hand along the dark wood of the banister. Katya's studio is nestled in a room that lies partially under the stairs just off the kitchen. Inside she grabs the same painting with the tree and holds it up to me.

"Focus on this tree," she says. I roll my eyes—not this again. "Just humor an old lady." Katya winks.

I look at the painting again, focusing on the detail in each stroke. Then my eyes play a trick on me again, and the leaves slightly move. I look back up at Katya.

"Try harder."

I stare at the center—the heart of the tree—ignoring my peripheral vision. The trunk is a combination of colors, representing the texture of the bark. Each flame formed by the turn of a paintbrush, the imagery so lifelike it starts to dance in front of my eyes as the hues begin to flow together. I can almost hear the cracking of the fire and the leaves rustling in the wind. Suddenly, the fire jumps out of the painting at me.

"What was that?" I scream as I jump backward.

"That is your destiny," Katya says.

"My *what?*"

"Your destiny. Your tea leaves speak of secrets. I cannot hold this one from you any longer. You will be seventeen on the eve of the autumnal equinox. It is not fair for you to find out everything then."

"How did that painting move?" I ask, still breathless.

"You summoned it." Katya stares back at me.

"What are you talking about?"

"You summoned what hides inside it," my great-aunt says more firmly. "The power is in your blood."

I stare at Katya, wondering if maybe Chantal was right: she's not all there.

"It means you are finally learning your heritage. This is what you were meant to be."

"You're crazy." I step back from Katya. "The town says you're just a fool. Mom always said her family made stuff up; that's why she kept me away from all of you. The entire family must be a bunch of liars!"

"That is not correct," Katya says, unyielding. "Your mother ran from her destiny, yet it haunted her to her last day. Like her, you are a summoner. Had she embraced it, she may still be here today."

"Shut up!" I yell. "You don't know what you're talking about!" I run from the room up to my bedroom and slam the door. Just to be safe, I drag my dresser in front of it.

I look around the room for some way to protect myself. A summoner? What's that supposed to mean? And what does it have to do with that painting or my mother? The urge to flee overtakes me. That's what's in my blood: the ability of flight. I need to get out of here. If I tell the authorities my great-aunt is senseless, maybe they'll send me back home to California where nothing is stable, but at least it's familiar. But I know that's not true. They'll simply send me to another long-lost relative, or some crappy foster care. I have no idea what I'm going to do. No. I need to take care of myself. I open my bedroom window, as a quiet knock raps on my door.

"Go away," I yell.

"Daciana—"

"Please just leave me alone." I crawl out the window, onto the roof of the front porch, and sneak to the side of the porch. There I climb down the vine-covered lattice, slipping out of the house onto the front lawn. It's an epic escape as far as I'm concerned.

As I peek about for my next route, I see Brennan's truck driving toward me. The last thing I need is to have to Brennan trying to question me with Katya. I duck onto a small path that runs between our house and the neighbor. I want to be left alone—by everyone.

The path takes me into the woods that run behind our street; they sit between our neighborhood and another one a few blocks away. It looks like it was the town's attempt to integrate nature into the community. The fall hues of orange and red intermingle with the green foliage yet to change, and those that have fallen, crunch under my feet with every step.

The paths here are strategically placed and made from crushed gravel. I decide to make my own path through the trees, and veer off to the right. I'm tired of trying to fit in, and it's only been one day.

After walking for a few minutes, I'm a little calmer and can think more clearly. If what I saw in Katya's studio was real, then what I saw in the bathroom was real. That means I summoned that little creature at the arcade. But what does that mean, *summoner*? I wish I were back at the house to ask Katya more questions.

Up ahead something moves, and I instantly think about the creature. Could it be here? Is it following me? More importantly, is it dangerous? I creep up to a tree and peer around its side to get a better look at what I'm dealing with.

What I see is not a tiny creature, crawling about, spying on me, no, not at all. It's Tryan executing some exercises between the trees, and he's not wearing a shirt. I watch him for a while, his muscles tensing with every action, his movements precise and filled with purpose; it's almost intoxicating. That or the whiskey is still settling in.

I shift my feet and snap a stick in the process. It cracks through the silence, like a tree falling. I stand still, frozen in place, as Tryan stops moving and looks straight at me.

"Did you get a good look?" he asks, walking over to me.

I shake my head, meaning to say no, but I'm too embarrassed to speak.

He stops in front of me. "Well, here you go." He crosses his arms over his chest. "Look all you want."

"I wasn't."

"So you weren't spying on me?"

"I thought you were something else." I spin on my heel and start to walk away.

"Wait," Tryan says, putting his hand on my shoulder. "What are you looking for? *Something* not someone?"

"It's nothing," I say, facing him. He has stubble on his chin, unlike most of the boys I've seen. His isn't sparse either, and it runs up his chin line to the end of his jaw. Something inside of me lets out a tiny sigh. "I was just trying to find somewhere to be alone."

"It doesn't sound like nothing," he says quietly, staring down at me. "But are the dark woods a good place for a girl like you to be alone?"

He tilts his head, looking at me with faint amusement, and his lips slightly curl on the one side. His lips—I can't stop staring at them. There's a pull between us, nothing I've ever felt before. Is Katya's reading coming true? Is this my romance? But it feels stronger, as if we're tied together, and tiny strings are pulling me closer to him. Suddenly, I lean forward, press my lips against his, and a spark goes off like earlier, only this time it's on the inside.

"Whoa," Tryan says, pulling back. "What are you doing?"

The strings between us snap, and I can't think. My face flashes hot, and my hand jumps to my lips, which are still parted and reverberating from the sensation of his mouth. Seconds pass and the spark slowly dies.

Ohmygawd. What am I doing? I turn again but this time break out into a run through the woods. My legs can't carry me fast enough.

"Wait, Dacie!" Tryan shouts after me.

But I don't stop running.

CHAPTER FIVE

Brennan's truck still sits outside of my house. I keep to the shadows until I'm out of view of the front window, then eye up the roof of the porch, contemplating how I might get back up without alerting anyone inside.

"It's not as easy getting up as it is getting down." Constantine's voice makes me jump out of my skin, as he comes up beside me. It's also the longest sentence I've heard him string together since we met.

"I was considering taking a different route to my room." I eye him up, waiting to judge his reaction. He doesn't flinch.

Up this close, I can see his leathery skin, broken apart by hundreds of lines from years of working in the sun. The crow's feet on either side of his eyes indicate he knows how to smile, though it's not something I've seen much of since I met him.

"Not in the mood for pleasantries?" he asks, raising one eyebrow.

"Not at all."

"Then I'd recommend a partner," he says, cracking a smile between his peppered goatee. "Let me usher you in, and I will deal with your great-aunt."

"I'd rather climb back up," I say sheepishly. "I kind of barricaded my door."

He lowers one brow, then nods and motions for me to follow him around the side of the house. The garden runs along here, reaching toward the back, where the yard disappears into the woods that sit behind the house.

He disappears into his workshop, and I glance inside. Along the interior wall hangs a variety of garden tools. A shiny one flashes at me from the sunlight. Hold on—was that a sword? He reappears with a ladder, blocking my view.

"Here," he says, passing me one end of the ladder as he closes the door behind him and locks it. I help carry the ladder to the front porch, where he holds it secure for me.

"No more climbing on roofs, okay?"

I nod and scramble back into my bedroom window.

"Daciana?" Katya calls from downstairs, as I stumble onto my floor. I hear Constantine come inside and say something as I climb onto my bed.

I lie back and think about Tryan; I can't believe I just kissed him. I've only ever kissed one other boy, and that was when I turned thirteen. My friends and I thought it would be a great idea to get drunk, so I stole a bunch of my mom's booze. I hardly remember the kiss, let alone the rest of the night; I was lucky more didn't happen. Mom was livid when she went to pour a drink the next morning, and her bar was dry. She made me sleep it off on the balcony and then we moved the next week. I wish we could move now, so I didn't have to face Tryan again.

Brennan's truck starts up, and I jump out of bed just in time to look through my window as it drives away. At least I don't have to deal with awkward conversations now.

A quiet knock interrupts my thoughts. Maybe I spoke too soon.

"Your friend has left," Katya says from the other side. "May I come in?"

"We need to discuss some things first."

"I feel terrible," she says, from the other side of my door. "That was an awful way for me to show you our powers; I apologize." She bursts into tears. "Oh please, Daciana, I don't know how to do this. I've never had children. I'm trying my best."

I pause, holding in the harsh words I had prepared for her. She never hesitated once when it came to taking responsibility for me—she deserves my respect. "Okay," I say, folding my hands on my pillow on my lap. "I'll open the door, but you have to stay out there."

"Agreed," she says, sniffling.

I push the dresser away and take a deep breath before opening my bedroom door. "You have five minutes." Katya flashes me a weak smile. I notice she's holding a small box in her hands. I step back into my bedroom and sit on the edge of my bed, facing her.

"What did your mother tell you about our family?" she asks.

"That none of you are safe."

Katya nods in understanding. "That can be true. What else?"

I try to swallow past a dry lump in my throat. "She told me not to trust any of you."

"Do you feel that way about me?" she asks. I shrug. "That makes me sad." She looks down at the box in her hands. "I knew your mother when she was young. She was my sister Bianca's daughter. Bianca would have been your grandmother."

"I've never heard of her," I say.

"That's because your mother ran away the day your grandmother died," Katya says, looking at me seriously. She motions to the box in her hands. "May I?" she asks. I nod.

She opens the box, and pulls a photo out from inside and holds it out to me. "Here is a photo of your mother, grandmother, and me. You may recognize the house in the background."

I slowly stand and take the photo from her, then return to my bed. It's a younger version of my mother, long before I was born. On one side of her is a younger Katya, though not so different looking than she is today. On the other side of my mother is a stern-looking woman with similar features to Katya, but broader. She must be my grandmother, Bianca.

Katya walks into my bedroom and joins me on the edge of my bed. "I am so sorry to upset you with all of this. That was not my intention."

"I just miss her."

"I know you do," she says. "But it is time you learn more about your family. You will be seventeen soon. In our family, one receives their full abilities at seventeen. It is dangerous for you not to learn before then."

I stand up and look out my bedroom window. Constantine is now at the front walk trimming the roses, and the ladder is gone. I can't imagine what he would have thought had I jumped off the roof in front of him. I might have given him a heart attack at his age.

"You said my mother ran from her destiny," I say. "I know she ran away from home but never understood why. What happened to her mother?"

"It was *Diavol*," Katya whispers.

The name gives me shivers as it rolls off my great-aunt's tongue.

"Who is he? A demon?"

Katya nods.

"Alina was pregnant with you when she accidentally let out Diavol, a very powerful demon whom she could not control. She tried to send him back, but he attacked her. Bianca stepped in to protect her. But Diavol was too strong, and he took her life."

"How did my mother get away?"

"No idea. Your mother was already gone by the time I got there, but the evidence remained; Alina's painting was ripped apart, and Bianca lay bleeding on the ground. With her last breath, Bianca spoke one word: '*Diavol*.'"

A cool breeze moves through my window. Just the mention of the name seemed to fill the bushes below with shadows. I slam my window shut and pull down the blinds. I've never seen the shadows gather like that.

"My mother felt responsible for her mother's death," I say with a pang of my own guilt.

I recall my memories of my mother. In my early youth, I remember finding her sitting in the kitchen, sadly staring out the window, smoking a cigarette with a half-empty bottle of vodka next to her. Then in the next moment, she would be spinning me around the kitchen, laughing and dancing the afternoon away.

When I got older, her drinking got worse. Sometimes I would get calls from the strip club she worked at to come pick her up in the morning before I went to school. She'd be slurring her words, and I'd have to carry her to the car, then to her bed. When I'd get home from school, I'd find her back at the table with another bottle of vodka, quietly staring outside again and the cycle could repeat for days. Eventually, she started bringing men home after work and at first that was embarrassing, but it became a relief not to have to see her intoxicated.

"I had a private investigator follow her as much as I could," Katya explained. "But they were always one step behind. It was as if Alina could tell when someone was coming after her, and she would take you and disappear into the night. It would take me months to locate you both again."

I smile at my mother's powers of evasion. I always thought she was simply flighty. She was an excellent runaway.

"Her drinking got worse over the years—as well as her dignity,"

Katya says sadly. "I wish I could have stepped in and saved you, but I had to stick to the oath."

"I didn't need saving," I say. "We had each other. Wait—what oath?"

"The family oath," Katya says. "We do not separate mothers from children—ever. No matter how dangerous the situation can be. Not even the Senate can, and they're in charge of upholding the laws of summoning."

"It wasn't dangerous," I mumble.

"I beg to differ," she says. "Look how it played out in the end."

The familiar sense of anxiety comes back to me. Whenever I think of my mother, the last night we had together always floods my thoughts. Two men hidden in the shadows. Me hidden under my mother's bed. But there wasn't enough time for her to hide. So she attacked them.

"Why didn't the Senate come after her? Not to separate us, but to question her?"

"Their power doesn't extend outside of Romania."

"So no one polices summoners in the other parts of the world?"

"There are other boards of authority—but no, we don't pay much mind to them. They aren't established like the Senate."

I don't want to talk about this anymore, but I want to know more about Diavol. I shake my head, trying to clear it of my memories and continue. "Did they catch Diavol after he killed my grandmother?" The word feels weird on my tongue. My mother never spoke of my grandmother—not once.

"Diavol disappeared," my great-aunt explains. "He is a terrible dark demon; one of the worst of all the supernatural. They do not pay much attention to the things of humankind. They usually stay low and feed off the power of others, stirring up lower demons and such to cause chaos in the world."

I think of the painting in Katya's studio. When I stared at the painting, the fire in the tree became alive. It tried to reach out to me. Was it real?

"Is that him in your painting?" I shudder.

"No, that is an Ifrit," she explains, "a simple fire demon. Diavol is still out there, somewhere."

"So I have to summon things like him?" A shiver runs down my spine. I can't fathom letting through evil demons, let alone being responsible for them.

"You have the ability to bring demons into this world," she says. "They are drawn to you because you are a gateway, but you also have an obligation to police them. That is if they get out of hand, you know, break the rules, that sort of thing."

"So we are like the demon police?" I ask. This is much weirder than I thought it could be.

"No," she says. "We are just responsible for the demons we let through. If one gets out of hand, then we have to deal with it. In our family, we send them back through our paintings."

"Why would we let any through in the first place?" I ask, thinking about the tiny creature at the arcade with dread. "Aren't demons just naturally bad?"

"We are responsible for keeping the balance," she says. "Without darkness, there cannot be light. Without evil, there cannot be good. This is our role."

"Why send them back then?" I ask. I can't believe I'm actually entertaining this idea. "Why not kill them?"

"Daciana!" Katya exclaims. "We are not killers—we are summoners. Do not forget that. To hunt demons is a punishable crime. It will do more harm than you could understand."

"What happens if we lose one?" I ask.

"Then we must do everything to find it," she says. "We are responsible for everything it does. The Summoner Guild back in Romania makes us accountable for all of our actions. If a demon we let through kills, and we do not attempt to retrieve it, then we can be held responsible for its crimes."

Now I'm worried about that tiny creature. Could something so small cause much trouble? "What if I refuse?"

"You may have already started seeing them reach out to you. They are like tiny streaks at first. Once you turn seventeen, you will see them in their true forms everywhere you go. You can ignore them, but they will just pester you until you listen."

I cross my arms. So I have no choice but to let them through. The rest of my life has already been predetermined. The severity of it all falls heavy on my shoulders.

"Would you like to come back to the studio now?"

I desperately want to say no, but my curiosity is too strong. "Yes."

I leave the safety of my bedroom and follow Katya to the studio.

Inside, everything looks normal, as it always has before. Paintings hang on the walls and easels throughout the studio. Most are covered. But the few that aren't, I'm able to look at, though careful not to linger too long for fear of releasing something terrible. The scenes seem so peaceful and innocent, but now I know each one is a portal to a horrendous place filled with evil and darkness.

"How does the summoning work?" I ask.

"You bring them through paintings," she explains. "Then, if need be, you paint them back into a painting to send them back."

"Is there one you can show me?" I ask. "Maybe one that's nice."

"None are inherently nice," she says. "Do not forget that, Daciana. All demons have the underlying sense to be evil. Some are just more so than others."

"And if they do something terrible, then it's on our conscience?" I ask, thinking of the imp that had disappeared into town.

"Sadly, yes," Katya agrees. "You will learn to live with that as well. Guilt subsides over time. It will make you a sharper summoner, to the point where you can almost predict their actions. The best of us can even manipulate them to use their powers."

"Use their powers?" I repeat. "How do you mean?"

"Take the Ifrit." She points back to the painting of the tree. "There are many Ifrits in the world, some more powerful than others. I have known this one a long time and therefore have let him out and locked him away on a number of occasions. Over time I came to understand him and his need to … burn." My great-aunt lifts her hands in a trance and fire appears in her palms. I gasp at the sight. As quickly as it appeared, she waves her hands, and the fire is gone. "We have an understanding now."

"How is that possible?"

"I summoned his power," she says.

At that moment, I know it's true. It's all true. The family I never knew, our abilities, and the responsibility I have awaiting me on my seventeenth birthday. I can feel my newfound power, somewhere deep inside. I see it in the shadows that follow me, and I witnessed it through the imp I let out.

My breath catches in my throat, and the room starts to feel too small. "It's all a bit much," I choke out.

"I understand," Katya explains. "There is still time. We're finished talking about this today. We will introduce a little bit each day to prepare you for your birthday."

I nod and return to my room, staring out the window. I am exhausted from running around, from talking about my mother, and from the information overload. It's a lot to take in. Is that why Mom ran away? Was it too much to bear to have this responsibility? Will I be able to handle it?

Something moves in the street below. Tryan is walking away with his own shadow chasing after him.

CHAPTER
SIX

At school the next day, I'm determined to ignore everyone I've
befriended. I'd rather be a nobody than be marked as the weird
girl. Making my way through the hallways unnoticed, I almost
manage isolation until Brennan sees me.

"Hey, Dacie!" he calls out after lunch. "I've been looking for you
all day. Did your aunt tell you I stopped by your place?"

"She did," I say, throwing my books in my locker and grabbing
my art supplies. I turn and move past Brennan. Tryan is up ahead,
waiting out front of Art while Chantal talks to him.

"Wait up." Brennan catches up and walks too close again. "So,
the school dance is tonight."

I keep walking, trying to get within earshot of Tryan and Chantal.
Brennan continues. "I was wondering if you wanted to go with me."

"What?" I stop on the other side of the door to Art.

"I said, 'will you go to the dance tonight with me'?" Brennan blushes.

Chantal laughs overly loud at Tryan, and then looks over at Brennan and me. I stare at Tryan, and he looks back at me all nonchalant. I can feel my heart flop into my stomach.

"Yeah, I guess," I say to Brennan. "*Only* if we all go as a group. I don't do dates."

"For sure," Brennan says. "Awesome! I'll pick you up at seven." He walks past Tryan and Chantal, beaming. Chantal glares at me and turns toward Tryan. "So, uh, do you have a date to the dance tonight?" She looks over at me and smirks.

"No." Tryan frowns, then turns around, disappearing into Art.

Chantal shrugs and chases after Brennan. Girls are stupid.

I slip into class just as the bell rings and slide into my chair. I avoid eye contact with Tryan, but it feels like his eyes burn into the back of me all through class. Halfway through class, he passes by my desk, slipping a piece of paper onto it. I watch as he hands in his project and leaves early.

I unfold the paper and find a sketch of me again. This time I'm staring out my bedroom window at a boy in the woods; the boy looks surprisingly like Tryan. Is he trying to tell me something? Between the trees behind him, something dark flits by, but I ignore it. I don't get it—why does Tryan care? One second he doesn't want me to kiss him, and in the next, he drawing pictures of me.

I go back to working on my drawing. Katya's discussion about the

Ifrit was on my mind all night. I start drawing a campfire, working hard on making the wood detailed enough before I start working on the flames. I think back to the flames that Katya's painting had. Hers were hues of yellows, oranges, and reds, but I'm just sketching with a pencil. I focus on the shapes, making some darker than others and erasing sections to show where the fire would burn brighter. I'm so focused on the drawing that I don't hear the bell ring.

I look up as people start gathering their things. An entire hour has gone by? How did that happen? A girl one row over waves her hands at me. "Whoa—your paper is smoking!" I look down, see black smoke rising from my sketch, and jump out of my chair. The girl screams. I grab my water bottle and dump it on the sketch. The smoke disappears, and the detailed lines and shading all begin to mesh into a mess of pulp and smudges.

"Dacie!" My art teacher appears at my desk. "You can't start fires in class!"

"But I didn't!"

I look up from the mess on my desk to try to extend a visual plea, but I only see her eyes heavy with disappointment as they stare down at me from under scrunched up eyebrows. She isn't about to understand and truthfully, I don't know how to explain it.

"Go to the principal's office right now!"

I scoop up my mess, as if hiding the evidence will make it go away. I dump it in the trash as I trudge out of class. As I head to the principal's office, I ignore everything around me: flirting cheerleaders, jovial jocks; it all seems so trivial. I didn't care about any of it before coming to Greystone High, but now that it's not my choice to be carefree like the rest of them, it's harder to block them out, happiness and all.

But really, how could I have been so stupid? I don't even know how I did it. I wasn't thinking about summoning a demon—I was just drawing fire. I need to get a hold on this ability before something bad happens.

Inside the office, the secretary motions for me to sit, and it's not long before the principal comes out to get me. I'm sure my teacher called up the second I left.

"Miss Cantar?" Principal Smyth motions me into her office. I grab the same seat I did when Katya brought me here for registration.

"So how are you settling in?"

Seriously. Is she going to skirt the issue? I prefer to get to the point. "I didn't start that fire." Well, it's almost true.

Principal Smyth raises an eyebrow. "How did it start then?"

"I don't know." I say, playing with a string on the bottom of my shirt.

She gets up from her desk and comes around to my side, sitting on the edge much closer to me than I'd like. "I understand things are hard with what you've gone through."

"It's not that." I look up at her and narrow my eyes. "Seriously. This wasn't me. Check my bag. Check my pockets. Check my locker." I stand up and dump my bag on her desk. It's a little brazen, but I'm determined to get out of here. "It must have been something combusting, what with all that paint thinner and dirty rags that the teacher leaves around the classroom."

Principal Smyth returns to her side of the desk and gestures for me to clean up my things. Her face looks unimpressed, and my cheeks heat up a little as I grab my personal things.

"I need to contact your aunt to come get you."

"Why?"

"I think it would be best if you went home for the rest of the day. You seem a little agitated; I think some quiet time is a good idea."

I slouch back in my chair. This sucks. Katya is going to be livid when she hears I was screwing around with demons. Smyth attempts to reach my great-aunt, but there's no answer.

"She doesn't believe in cell phones." I smirk. At least Katya's off-the-grid lifestyle will serve me well for once.

"You can wait in the counseling room while I try to reach her."

I'm ushered to the other side of the office, passing by the secretary again. She doesn't bother to look up. I'm sure she has bigger problems than me.

Inside the counseling room, I run my finger along the brochures. One side of the office is filled with college applications, and the other side has pamphlets on suicide, teen pregnancy, and addiction. Wow. What a combination.

I grab one of the college applications. When I lived with Mom, this seemed like my only escape to a normal life. Go to college and live on campus, fleeing Mom and her destructive lifestyle. Now will this ever be a choice? Does a summoner get to choose a career?

"Looking at your future?"

I jump at the unfamiliar voice and spin around. A woman is standing there, leaning against the door to the counselor's office. She's dressed conservatively in a pencil skirt, and white blouse, and her long tight curls bounce from her head and frame her smooth dark brown skin. Suddenly, I feel underdressed.

"Not really," I say as I toss the brochure back on the rack and slump into a chair.

"You're new here, aren't you?" she says, and I nod. "One sec." She disappears into her office and then reappears with a file. "You're Daciana, right?"

"Dacie," I say.

"How do you like the town so far?"

I shrug and try not to make eye contact. "It's okay, I guess."

"I was going to find you yesterday," she says. "But I thought it was better to give you some space."

"Why did you want to see me?"

"I like to meet all the new students." She smiles. "I'm Miss Nelson, the guidance counselor."

"What does that file say about me?" I ask, wondering if reports from California made it all the way here. Phrases like *socially withdrawn,* and *emotional detachment* come to mind from my last counseling session.

"Nothing yet." She holds the folder out to me. "Want me to add something?"

I shake my head and smile, about to look up at her as the secretary comes in. "You can go back to classes, Dacie."

"Seriously?"

"Be good." Miss Nelson winks.

In the cafeteria, Brennan stands up waving his hands in the air at me. I hesitate as I quickly glance over the occupants: Zack, Sophie, and no Chantal. I make my way through the crowd.

"I heard you got in trouble in art," Brennan says as I sit down. "Are you still allowed to go to the dance?"

I shrug. "The principal didn't say."

Brennan's face relaxes. "Good."

"Where's Chantal?" Even though I don't want to see her, her absence is rather odd.

Brennan rolls his eyes. "Who knows? I asked to borrow her notes after first period, and she flipped out on me. I think she has a crush on that new guy from your Art."

"Who, Tryan?" I can feel my pulse begin to race at the thought of them together.

"Yeah," he continues, "she's been asking around about him, and this morning I saw her throwing herself at him."

I shake my head. "I think you're wrong."

"Well, whether I am or not, that's their problem." He turns back to Zach and Sophie. "You guys want to double date with Dacie and me?"

I glare at Brennan. "It's not a date, remember."

He shrugs, but I feel myself backed into a corner. How could I be so naïve? "You know what? I need to go home early tonight, so I'll just meet you guys there."

"What?" Brennan looks shocked, and I'm sure I catch Zack hiding a smirk out of the corner of my eye.

"Yeah, sorry. This whole fire thing, you know."

"This sucks." Brennan starts to play with his food, and I have the satisfaction of being back in control of my life again. Now if I could only extend some of that to my new abilities, everything would be better.

CHAPTER
SEVEN

I head home and look through my closet for something to wear to the dance. It's sparse, to say the least; I've never needed anything more than a T-shirt and jeans before. A box of my mother's things pokes out from under some bags at the back of my closet. All she owned were skirts, dresses, and other revealing items. I pull out the box and find the least revealing one at the bottom: a simple black cocktail dress. Perfect.

Downstairs I seek out Katya to help me get the wrinkles out of the dress. It'll be amusing to see the shock on her face when I tell her I'm going out for the second night in a row. I can't find her in the kitchen, so I go into her studio. She's not here either, but something feels strange, so I look around.

Toward the back of the studio, there's a large easel covered in broadcloth. I pull off the cloth, and find a half-finished painting underneath. The scene is a dark city street with a lamp illuminating one area. There's nothing else in the street.

I practice my talent and stare at the painting, focusing on the street. For a moment, the figure of a man appears, standing in the distance. I gasp and blink, but when I look back, he's gone.

"Daciana?" Katya calls from the front entry. "Are you home?"

I quickly cover the painting back up and hurry out of the studio. I nearly run into my great-aunt and Constantine in the kitchen. He's got a large sword, which usually hangs in our study, lying across the table as he sits polishing it.

"What were you doing in there?" Katya asks, as she puts away groceries. That's one thing I can give her credit for—she keeps the house well stocked with food. I put the dress on the counter and help them out.

"I was looking for you," I say. "There's a school dance tonight, and I'm going."

"That's fantastic!" Katya says, clapping her hands and running over to kiss my cheeks. "We need to go shopping for something to wear."

"I found this dress of Mom's." I point to the counter. "Can you help me get ready?"

"Of course!" Katya says. She looks like she's in heaven.

After what feels like hours of primping, I'm impressed with the outcome. Katya has added soft curls to my long dark hair, and applied makeup to my pale face. My mother used to dress me up when I was little, but as I got older, I avoided it completely, not wanting her to turn me into her. The fact that she won't see me like this makes my heart twinge a little, and brings a tear to my eye.

"A Cantar lady never cries, dear," Katya says. "Hold your head high and your emotions in. There, look at you. Perfection."

I look back at the mirror and swallow down my tears before they can show. Maybe this won't be so bad after all. I go downstairs and Constantine is waiting for me at the table; he looks up and nods in approval at my makeover. I quickly eat some supper while waiting for Brennan to pick me up.

"What's this boy like?" Katya asks.

"You met him," I say between mouthfuls.

"Yes," she says, "but he wouldn't let me read his leaves—polite otherwise. What do you know of his family?"

"Nothing." I laugh, almost choking on my food.

"This is no laughing matter," she explains. "Family line is important. You can't just pair up with the first person you come across."

"Pair up?" I say. "What century is this? Listen, Brennan might be interested in me, but the feeling is not mutual."

"Then why get all dressed up?"

"I just thought it would feel nice to be like everyone else," I say, looking down at my food.

"Is that what has been going on?" Katya exclaims. "My dear, you will never be like everyone else. You are much too special."

"Thanks," I grumble, looking up from my food, "that makes me feel real—" I stop in the middle of my sentence and almost drop my fork when I see the missing imp crawling on the window outside the kitchen.

"Don't mumble," Katya says. "It's not polite."

"I have to run," I say, standing up from the table.

"I've told you," Katya lectures, "here we ask to be excused from the table, and what about your date?"

"I'm meeting him at the dance," I say, grabbing my bag and running out the back door.

Outside, I scan the side of the house for the imp, but it's not there. I run out into the backyard, searching for the creature. "Hello?" I call out.

"Shhh," a voice says from behind the trees at the edge of the woods. "Over here."

Its hairy claws and twisted face peer out from behind a tree. I run over to it, keeping a safe distance. "What are you doing here?"

"Why didn't you come after me before?" the imp asks.

"I didn't know I was supposed to."

"What are you, some newbie?" the imp says, looking me up and down. "You are, aren't you?" I fold my arms, not sure what to admit to this creature. "Well, you're in luck; I need you to send me back right now."

I shake my head. I refuse to admit to this *thing* that I have no idea how to do that.

"Are you serious?" Its eyes grow wide. "What kind of summoner are you?"

"One with somewhere to be," I say. "Hang out here, and I'll find you when I get back. Oh, and be quiet, or my great-aunt will find you."

"That might be too late!" it says. "It's not safe out here. I need to go back. Send me back right now!"

The imp lunges at me, and I grab it by its shoulders, holding it out from me as it kicks and bites at me. Thankfully, my arms are longer than it is, so it can't connect. The creature is no heavier than a large cat. I carefully carry it over to my little car and pop the hatch open. Inside, I wrap the little creature in a blanket, securing it with my booster cables.

"Let me go," it screams as it wiggles. I close the hatch to stifle the sound and climb in the driver's seat.

"Don't worry," I say. "I'll figure this out after the dance."

CHAPTER EIGHT

The decorations in the school gym are beyond anything I could have imagined. Lights bounce off glitter-filled balls that spot the ceiling like a faux night sky. Lasers shoot out from the corners, emitting multi-colored streams of light to the pulse of the music. A DJ sits on the stage, looking down from behind his throne of speakers and turntables while his beats rebound off the walls. This is my first time at a school dance. It looks pretty cool.

I move along the edge toward groups of people, trying to see if I can spot Tryan anywhere. Maybe he's not coming. I should've expected that this wouldn't be his thing. *What's he doing right now?* I start to think about the kiss in the woods, when Brennan interrupts my thoughts.

"Oh, come on," Brennan teases. "Dance with me. Just one song?"

He puts on a pouty face and makes me laugh.

"Okay, but just one."

He grabs me by the hand and pulls me out onto the dance floor. I've heard this slow tune many times before on the radio. I'm glad I recognize it.

As Brennan pulls me closer, he smiles at me. Chantal is watching us intently from the wall of the gym. I wish she'd realize we're just friends, but I'm not sure Brennan feels the same.

As Brennan spins me around, I see other familiar faces. Sophie and Carter are dancing close by. Miss Nelson isn't far off, mingling with students, probably making sure no one's groping. And then I see him: Tryan. He's watching us from the other end of the school gym. He's not just watching; he's staring. My breath catches in my throat as I remember our kiss the other night—the kiss that sparked the neighborhood.

He starts to walk toward us and as he gets behind Brennan, I stop dancing. I can feel that same pull I've felt every time we get close. It's almost like there's magnetism between us. I grunt at the pun, and Brennan looks at me confused; then Tryan taps his shoulder.

"May I cut in?" Tryan asks as he takes my hands, not waiting for Brennan to answer. I barely notice Brennan as he stands there looking confused before Chantal runs out to save his pride.

"Lovely night for a dance," Tryan whispers to me with his accent. A shiver runs down my spine.

"Yes," I manage to whisper back.

"Are you cold?" he asks.

I shake my head, unable to say anything more. His touch against my hands and his body moving mine along makes me feel on fire so that I can barely breathe, let alone speak. And I can't stop staring into his face.

"I've been thinking about you," he says quietly.

"You have?"

"You're surprised?" he says. "Well, I'll admit I'm a little surprised as well. I've never had someone stuck in my head like this before. Then there was that kiss. It was something else." He spins me around, slightly lifting my feet from the floor, pulling me against his body. My stomach knots in butterflies from the sensation. The song ends as I land.

"Thank you for the pleasure of this dance," Tryan whispers in my ear, and I close my eyes at the sensation of his breath. When I open them, he's still staring at me as he begins to walk away. Our hands are still touching, stretching out, until at last our fingers part and I feel the bond snap apart.

A new song comes on and the dance floor between us crowds with people. Before I can move again, he's gone.

"What was that about?" Brennan says from behind me. I turn and see Chantal with him.

"I don't know." I shake my head from the daze.

"I think he seriously likes you," Chantal says, watching my face. Hers looks relieved that my attention is somewhere away from Brennan. I think about Tryan again: his touch, his breath, his kiss. The gym is suddenly too small and it's hard to breathe. "I'll be back,"

I say, running past dumbfounded Brennan and Chantal's look of glee.

Miss Nelson is standing near the doorway. A look of worry crosses her brow as I approach her. "Are you okay, Dacie?"

"I just need some fresh air."

She nods. "This way."

She pulls me into the lighted foyer of the school and out the double doors at the front. I sharply turn and lay my back against the cold brick of the exterior. I stretch my fingers along the rough texture as I take deep breaths, trying to hold myself up for fear of fainting. *What is this feeling I get from being around Tryan?* It's as if I can't control myself.

"Just breathe," Miss Nelson says. "Did something happen in there? It looked like you were having fun when I saw you dancing."

How am I supposed to explain my feelings to her? I barely understand them myself.

"It was just so stuffy," I say. "I've never been to a dance before."

"Is that it?" She laughs. "It gets better, trust me. Want to take a walk around the school, then go back in? I'll join you."

"No." I shake my head. I feel drained. "I'm just going to go home."

"You know where my office is if you ever need to talk."

I quickly gather myself together and walk to my car. I can't go back in the gym like this. If I see Tryan again, what will I say to him? I'll look like a fool, stumbling over my words. Plus, Miss Nelson is nice, but she suffocates me with her attention.

As I walk into the school parking lot, I notice a dark blur run between two cars. I was so caught up in the school dance I forgot about the imp.

"Hey!" I quickly run after the creature. He's standing at the end of the two cars laughing at me. Suddenly, I forget all my angst from the dance.

"I told you to stay in the car," I whisper firmly. The imp jumps up and down on the spot then runs behind the cars. "Come back here!"

The imp darts around and jumps on top of the vehicles in the parking lot. "I warned you," he says. "I really, really did. I told you not to leave me, but you just had to go to your little human *dancie-dance*. Well, I need to get back. It's not safe out here. Something's off. Something's not right. Take me back right now!"

"That's what I'm trying to do," I say, exasperated.

"How do I know you mean it this time?" he asks with his eyes narrowed, staring at me from the hood of a car.

"You'll just have to trust me." I lunge at him, landing on the hood as he runs over the cab toward the back. "Get back here, you little—"

"Missing something?" Tryan appears from the back of the car. He's holding up the imp by the scruff of its collar.

"You let me down right now," the imp yells. "If you don't, you'll be sorry."

"I don't think so," Tryan says, turning the imp face-to-face with him. He stares the creature down and for a moment, something flickers in Tryan's eyes, but he's too far away for me to see.

"Oh, no!" the imp cries out. "Save me summoner! Save me! Don't let this evil tovaros kill me. Save me, *pleeeeease!*"

"What are you doing?" I ask Tryan. I'm shocked that not only is he holding the imp, but he's not surprised to see it.

"I'm catching him for you," Tryan says. "What I want to know is how you let this little guy out before your seventeenth birthday?"

CHAPTER NINE

I look awkwardly at Tryan, processing his words, and wondering how he can stand there so calmly. The imp kicks at him and tries to bite at his arm, but Tryan holds it straight out, unflinching. His arm span beats mine, easily.

I'm confused more than anything. "How do you know about this stuff?" I motion toward the imp.

"I know a lot more than you give me credit for," Tryan says. "Now, where'd you park?"

Tryan sits in the backseat of my car with the imp, whom he's strapped in beside him. The creature doesn't stop wiggling about, and I can't help but laugh from the front seat when I look in the rearview mirror.

"Don't you touch me, you evil tovaros," the imp hisses. "I know what you are. I know what you've done. I can see all your conquests through your eyes and smell death on your skin. You are very bad indeed."

A shadow falls over Tryan's face. "I'm not going to hurt you," he says, his voice filled with regret. "I'm going to make sure Dacie sends you back where you belong."

"She doesn't even know what she's doing," the imp complains. "What if she paints me into an ocean and I drown—or worse, what if she paints me into a bottle? I'll be stuck in there for eternity granting wishes to every future summoner that lets me free!"

"Well obviously you're going to have to help a little," I say to the creature.

"I know the laws of summoning," Tryan says quietly. "I'll help you."

"Ah, yes," the imp says. "You expect me to trust my life in the hands of an assassin."

"Are you a summoner, too?" I ask Tryan, ignoring the complaints of the imp.

"Sort of," Tryan says, avoiding my eyes in the rear-view mirror, looking out the window. "Will we be able to get into your aunt's studio?"

"How do you know about that?"

"I've dealt with things like this before."

"How long have you been doing this?" I ask.

"Four years," he says, still staring out the window.

"For all of high school?" I ask, shocked.

"I'm not seventeen, Dacie," he says. "Which brings me back to my first question, how did *you* do this before your birthday?"

"I have no idea how I did this, it just happened," I say. "And what do you mean you're not seventeen? How old are you?"

"I'm nineteen," Tryan says, glancing up at the mirror, watching my reaction.

"What are you doing in high school?"

"I missed a lot of classes last year hunting down things like this." He motions to the imp.

"You hunt them?"

"Used to," Tryan says. "Look, right now we need to get this thing back where it belongs. I'll answer all your questions later."

"Promise?" I ask, staring at him in the rear-view mirror.

Tryan finally meets my eyes and smiles at me. "Yes."

"How heartwarming." The imp speaks up from the back seat. "But let's hurry up. I'm running out of time."

I pull into the driveway next to my dark house. Thankfully, Katya and Constantine must have gone out—it's too early for them to have gone to bed. I breathe a sigh of relief. The last thing I need is to have to answer uncomfortable questions.

Tryan grabs hold of the imp, carrying it under his arm, as I open the front door and turn on the lights. We slip into the house and enter Katya's studio.

As I click on the lights, the imp gasps at the large number of paintings in it.

"*Mai!*" the imp gasps. "Your aunt is either a collector or a master;

do you know which?"

I shrug; I don't know the meaning of either. "She's painted these all, if that's what you mean."

"*Aoleu!*" the imp exclaims again. "She's a master then. What's your family name?"

"That's none of your business," Tryan says, pushing the imp farther into the room.

"Hey!" the imp cries out.

"Don't be mean," I say to Tryan, who shoots me a confused look. "He's here; he obviously wants to cooperate."

"You don't understand," Tryan explains. "He might look tiny and helpless, but imps aren't—they're sneaky, and they like to play pranks and spy on people."

The imp speaks up. "I was good this time. There were no pranks, I promise." He looks up at me, pleading. "I just want to go back; I want to be safe."

"Safe from what?" Tryan asks.

"From out there," the imp says, hiding behind my leg.

"Don't lie to me," Tryan says, "I know your kind; you can't wait to get out of the netherworld. Why do you want to get back there so bad?"

"I think my new friend will let me out when I'm ready," the imp says, tugging on my dress. "Right?"

"Tell me the truth," Tryan says, "or I won't show your summoner how to put you back."

The imp steps out from behind me and crosses his arms. He

stares at Tryan with narrowed eyes and sticks out his lower lip as he taps his foot on the wooden floor. "Fine!" he says, losing patience. "I ran into another demon. He was being a big bully and wouldn't let me have any fun. He warned me to go back home and come back out with someone else."

"What's that supposed to mean?" Tryan asks. "This demon knows Dacie?"

"It means he's a real jerk," the imp says. "I told him this town doesn't have his name written on it, and you know what he did? He tried to kill me, just over a simple disagreement!"

"Demons don't kill imps," Tryan says. "They could care less about you guys. You must have been in his way."

"I don't care what you say, tovaros," the imp snarls. "I told the truth. Now send me back."

Tryan crosses his hands, about to argue, but I step in. "Someone tell me what to do. We need to hurry before Katya gets home."

"Get a painting ready," the imp says, "and then paint me into it."

"How do I know which are empty?" I ask, looking around the room. My eyes settle on the burning tree, and I remember the fire creature that leaned out toward me. I quickly look away from it.

"You should be able to tell by looking at it," he says. "You're the summoner."

"How about this one?" Tryan asks, pointing to one of an open pit.

"No way!" the imp squeals. "I want something nice." It looks around. "Like this one." It points toward a scenic painting of a mountain with a lake below it.

"That's nice," I begin. "But how do I know it's available?"

"Look for shadows," Tryan says. "That's where they hide."

I stare deep into the painting, waiting to see if anything moves. Nothing does. I step back and shrug.

"Good," the imp says. "Send me there."

"I still think you should send him to the pit," Tryan says. "Then if we need more answers, we know where to find him."

"No, no, no." The imp runs back behind my leg.

"It's fine," I say. "Let's just get this over with."

Tryan takes the painting down, and the imp sits beside it. I stare at them both, confused. "What am I supposed to do now?"

"Here," Tryan says, passing me a brush and a paint tray. "Paint the imp and connect him to the painting."

"What if I do it wrong?" I ask, getting nervous.

"If you can summon him out, you should be able to send him back," Tryan assures me. "Go ahead and try."

"Put me somewhere nice," the imp asks. "Like behind a tree. No one looks behind a tree."

I listen to the imp. This is all confusing. It makes about as much sense as the first time Katya told me I was a summoner. I sigh, dipping the brush into some brown paint, and start painting the imp's feet. *What else can I do?* Sweat breaks out on my forehead.

"Can you open the window for me?" I ask Tryan as I wipe my brow with the back of my hand.

"That tickles," the imp snorts as I run the brush along his foot.

Tryan rolls his eyes at the imp, then does as I ask.

I continue up the imp's pants to his torso, then switch over to some green paint. He looks content sitting there while I paint across his face over his head.

"Now," Tryan says, "you need to link him to the painting. Go ahead and draw on the floor right onto the painting, trust me."

I look at Tryan skeptically. This just gets weirder and weirder. But I do as he says and as soon as my brush stroke reaches the painting, the imp begins to squeal. "Thank you," he says as he leaps toward the painting, disappearing into its canvas. Suddenly, a tree appears where I touched the painting, and a long shadow stretches out from it. I jump back in surprise and drop my brush to the ground.

"It's okay," Tryan says, grabbing the painting. "You did it."

"I did?" I say, watching as he hangs it back on the wall.

"You did what?" Katya's voice calls out from behind us. Both Tryan and I jump around as Katya enters the room with Constantine. "What's going on in here?"

CHAPTER TEN

Katya looks from me to Tryan, then raises her hands in the air, waiting for an answer. Her bracelets clink together as they slide up her arms, stopping mid-forearm.

"I was just showing my friend what you do," I stammer.

"Really?" Katya says, pursing her lips together. "Tell me, who is this friend of yours?"

"My name is Tryan," he says, stepping forward and holding out his hand.

"Is that a Romanian accent?" Katya asks, raising one eyebrow and crossing her arms over her chest. Constantine awkwardly reaches in front of her and shakes Tryan's hand.

"Yes, ma'am," he says.

"And what interest do you have in my studio, tovaros?" she says, narrowing her eyes and staring Tryan down.

I freeze at the sound of that word again. *Tovaros*. What does it mean? First, the imp, and now Katya. I can tell by the way that Tryan's back goes rigid that he's hiding something.

"You think I was born yesterday?" Katya says. "I can see it all over you. How many summoners have you met before?"

"Many," Tryan says, clearing his throat and awkwardly rubbing his arm. I step closer to them, but he avoids looking at me. "I grew up in Romania."

"And how many have you served?" she asks.

Tryan hesitates, as he looks intently back at Katya. I look to Constantine, trying to get some understanding of what's going on here, but he's watching Tryan carefully as well.

"One," Tryan finally says. "Just this last year."

"Am I to assume she is gone now?" Katya asks.

Tryan nods.

Katya shakes her head. "I can only guess why you are around our little Dacie, but she is not seventeen yet, and her circumstances are special."

"I see that," Tryan says.

Katya frowns and looks at the painting on the wall behind Tryan before speaking again. "I forbid any further contact until after her birthday."

"Katya!" I cry out. I'm not sure why I care so much, but it seems a little drastic and none of her business.

"He knows much more about our world than you do," Katya warns.

Tryan still won't look in my direction. His hands are at his sides, balled into fists, and his jaw clenches, but he slowly lets go and says, "Fine."

"No!" I say. "You don't run my life. My mother never did and you sure as hell aren't going to start now."

"You should go," Katya says quietly.

Tryan nods his head and looks over at me. "I'm sorry, Dacie." He turns and walks out of the room with Constantine.

I stand frozen and confused. What just happened here? I look back at Katya, who's glaring at me. "Was that really necessary?" I ask.

She shakes her head, clearly angry. "Do you have any idea who he is?"

"He's a boy from Art."

"He's a tovaros," she says. "A summoner's companion. I imagine he's hanging around you, trying to see if there's a connection."

"I don't date," I remind her.

"He doesn't want to date," she mocks. "He wants to see if you have a connection."

"I'm not like my mom. I don't throw myself at any guy who shows an interest."

"Your mother!" Katya laughs. "She wanted nothing to do with her tovaros. She rejected the life of a summoner."

"Maybe she was the smart one."

"Don't you ever wonder why she was so impulsive?" Katya asks with more concern. "You can't run from this life; the demons will always find you. They're always lurking in the shadows whether you want to see them or not. Your mother tried to hide it all with booze, but in the end it found her."

"What did?" I ask.

Katya waves her hands in the air. "All this," she says. "It will eventually catch up with you. The weight of the responsibility will play games with your mind unless you can find your companion to share the load."

"Is that who my father was?" I ask. "Her tovaros?"

"Your mother never found her true tovaros," Katya says sadly. "And that was her undoing in the end."

We are interrupted by Constantine's entrance back into the room. "It's getting late," he says, smiling at me.

"Yes," she says. "Conversations like these are better served in the morning."

I turn to leave and see Katya walk over to the wall where Tryan hung the painting with the imp. She reaches up and straightens the painting, then turns back with a frown on her face. I quickly scoot out of the studio and up the stairs to my room before she can ask any more questions.

I try to turn in, but too much has gone on tonight. I think about Tryan and the look on his face when he caught the imp. *Is Katya right? Did he come here looking for me?* Finally, I fall asleep, but my dreams are haunted by the same nightmare I've had for six months. At the end of the dream, when everything goes silent, and I'm cowering under my Mom's bed, I hear a low whisper.

"*Dacie.*"

Wait, that never happened.

"*Dacie,*" it calls out to me again.

Slowly, I open my eyes and realize I'm not dreaming anymore. I'm under the covers in my bedroom at my great-aunt's house.

I sit up in bed; my head is pounding from the intensity of my nightmare. I get up and go downstairs to the kitchen to hunt for some aspirin. Katya's medicine cabinet is full of natural remedies like peppermint, basil, and other herbs and plants. I can't remember which combination she prefers, but I do remember seeing Constantine stuff a jar of aspirin in the back—after rummaging around, I find it.

I toss two pills into my mouth and gulp back some water as I stand at the kitchen sink, watching the rain spotting the outside of the window above it. The wind has picked up, and it blows the trees around. I smile, recalling the sight of the imp crawling on the outside of the house hours earlier. He was kind of funny; I don't know why Tryan was so mean to him.

"*Daaaacie.*"

I startle at the sound, much clearer now, and almost drop my glass. I spin around, but there's nothing behind me. I set my glass down and steady myself. The door to Katya's studio slowly creaks open, and I remember we left the window open in there.

I slip into the studio, well aware of the paintings surrounding me. *Are they full of demons? Do they know I'm in here?* As I make my way to the window, my mind plays tricks on me while shadows dance about in the corners of the room.

"*Daaaacie.*"

The sound comes from the curtains covering the open window. They're blowing wildly into the studio and the rain puddles underneath. It's just the wind. Katya won't be happy if she sees this.

I get to the window and have to pull hard to get it to shut as its wooden frame has swelled a little from the rain. Finally, it connects at the bottom, and I close the curtains just as a crack of lightning breaks through the air. I stifle a scream as the figure of a man appears, silhouetted through the curtains.

I step back, slipping on the puddle of water, and fall on my side. Scrambling, I try to get a foothold, and when I do, I run to the doorway of the studio and turn back to make sure nothing is following me. The silhouette is gone, but the deep whisper returns. This time it's longer: "*Daaaciana.*"

I slam the door to the studio and run up to my bedroom, sliding the dresser in front of my bedroom door and jumping under my covers. There's no way I'm moving until daylight returns.

CHAPTER ELEVEN

I drag my feet to the school the next day in a daze from my night. Katya woke me up after what felt like a couple of hours sleep at the most. She wasn't impressed that my door was barricaded, but didn't ask for an explanation.

"Dacie!" Brennan's voice comes from our lockers. "Over here!"

I grudgingly make my way through the crowd of students toward Brennan. When I get through Chantal is there hanging out next to him. She shoots me a quick smirk, but I ignore her and open my locker.

"What happened to you at the dance?" he asks. "I went looking for you, but you were gone."

"He saw you drive off with someone in your car." Chantal smirks.

"Have you seen Tryan?" I ask, ignoring the jibe.

Brennan looks at me, surprised. "Yeah, I think he's in the music room."

"Thanks," I say, throwing my books in my locker and slamming the door shut.

"Wait," he says, almost pleading. "I was wondering if you wanted to come watch football practice after school."

"Hmm?" I say, barely listening. "Football? Sorry, Brennan. It's not really my thing."

Chantal's smirk has changed into an unattractive grin and Brennan looks like I just punched him in the stomach. I don't have time for pleasantries; I'm looking for answers.

Miss Nelson stops me at the end of the hallway.

"Where are you storming off to?" she says, holding a hand up to me.

"I, uh, have to get something in the music room." My words come out weak and lame, but to my surprise, she nods.

"Make it quick," she says. "It's almost the bell."

I enter the stairwell, which is usually echoing with students avoiding class as long as they can. The only echoes right now are my sneakers on the stairs, as I run down three flights to the basement. Music lies at the end of the hallway past art. At the far end is drama. For some reason, they decided to stick all the Arts classes where there's no sun.

The teachers must be running behind, because the lights are still off down here. A red glow flanks the darkness of the hallway from the two exit signs at either end. I step forward and pause at the edge of the darkness. For a second I think I see a shadow move, but then I realize how stupid that sounds. How can darkness have shadows? I step forward and make my way to the music room.

A faint tune meets my ears. Someone is inside the room playing the piano. I recognize the piece—sometimes I caught my mother listening to it. It's Beethoven's "Moonlight Sonata." I lean back in the darkness against the cold cinder block wall, and close my eyes, remembering how my mother used to sway to the haunting music with her eyes closed. I always imagined she was thinking of happier times in her past.

One time she opened her eyes, and caught me watching her.

"Don't stare," my mother said in a drunken slur. "It's not ladylike."

She burst into fits of laughter, and I ran to my room and hid under the covers, embarrassed that I ever believed she cared about anything beautiful.

I shake my head, clearing it of my past, and turn with determination toward the door. But something moves by the art room. It looked like a person, but now they've disappeared into the darkness. I freeze and can only hear my heartbeat, thundering in my ears. I squint, and look down the hall. Is there really anything there? Shadows maybe—but are my eyes just playing tricks on me? I start to step toward it but then hear a shuffle against the vinyl floor, and I jump forward instead, exploding through the entrance of the music room, where Tryan is sitting at the piano. *Was that him playing?* I peek out the open doors behind me, but nothing follows.

Tryan stops playing and looks up from the piano.

"Why did you leave last night?" I don't wait for pleasantries. I came here on a mission.

He frowns. "I thought I better go. Your aunt didn't look too pleased."

"You left me alone."

"It *is* your house," Tryan says. "I'm sure you've been alone in there before."

"That's not the point." I throw my hands in the air.

Tryan gets up from the piano bench and slowly walks toward me. His T-shirt clings to his chest, showing he's more muscular than I realized. Thoughts of his bare chest enter my mind. I shake my head quickly, and hold my hand up to him.

"Stop," I say. "I need answers."

Tryan puts his hands up submissively. "At your service."

A shiver runs down my spine. He's too content to be the brooding loner I took him for at first sight. I walk past him and lean against the piano. Suddenly, words fail me, and I awkwardly fiddle with my hands.

"You *need* answers?" Tryan says, standing in front of me.

"I want to know what happens when I turn seventeen," I say, looking up at him and staring at his eyes.

"You'll be able to summon demons," he says, a smile playing at the edge of his lips. He likes this a little too much.

"But I already can," I say. "You saw that."

"Yes I did," Tryan says, tapping a finger on his lips. "I thought about that all night."

"You did?" My heart skips a beat.

"That and other things," he says, his lips twitching into a smile once again. "Your mother must have told you the incorrect birthday."

"That's it?" I roll my eyes. "That's stupid. Why would she do that?"

"Yeah," he says, shaking his head. "I didn't think it made sense either."

"Then how can I?" I ask.

"I've never heard of it," Tryan says. "You shouldn't be able to summon until you're seventeen. You should just see their shadows."

"You know more than I do about all this stuff. You're my only hope. Show me more."

"I really can't help," Tryan says. "I can't summon—I can just see the demons."

"Is that because—" I begin, ready to ask the real question I have for him, "you're a tovaros?"

Tryan smiles a little. "I thought you didn't know about these things?"

"Katya told me you help out summoners. It's your duty."

"It's more than that," Tryan says, leaning against the piano next to me. He closes his eyes and runs his hands through his hair. One arm rubs against mine as he shifts to cross his arms over his chest. The hair on my arm tingles from the sensation.

"What do you mean?"

Tryan turns toward me and looks at my face, starting at my chin, and moving up to my eyes. I can barely breathe, as I wait in anticipation for the answer.

"A tovaros is always looking," Tryan explains. "It's their job to seek out a summoner and be their companion."

There's that word again: *companion*. He said he had a summoner before. *Is he taken?*

"Why won't you help me then?" I ask.

"The relationship is complicated," Tryan explains. "Once a tovaros commits to a summoner, they're bonded together until death."

"What do you mean?" I ask. "Like soul mates?"

"If they're the perfect match, then yes." He nods, looking over at me again.

He told Katya he's met many summoners—were they all his soul-mates? I look back at his face, and it looks sad.

"So," I say quietly, "you can't help me because you're worried I might be your soul-mate?"

Tryan bursts out laughing, and my face instantly goes red. Then I start laughing with him. It does sound ridiculous aloud.

"That's not it at all," he says. "I'm more worried about what your great-aunt will do to me."

I lean my head back on the piano and put my hands over my face, speaking between my fingers. "I feel stupid."

"Don't," Tryan says. "If a summoner and a tovaros are a perfect match, they become stronger against demons. Your great-aunt just wants you to be careful; that's all."

"What happens if they're not a perfect match?" I ask.

"Then usually one of them ends up dead," Tryan says seriously.

"That imp seemed cute to you, but if he needed to, he would have ripped out your throat in a second. Don't let them fool you, Dacie. There's a reason that demons need to be monitored and there's a reason a summoner needs a tovaros."

A shiver runs down my spine. Is it fear or the fact that Tryan cares whether I get hurt or not? I look back at him, and he has that sad look again. Has he lost someone he loved?

"I really do need your help," I say. "Something has been calling out to me from Katya's studio. It knows my name, and I need to make it stop. Either you can do it with me, or I'm going to do it alone."

"Fine," Tryan says. "But we need to avoid your great-aunt."

CHAPTER TWELVE

We wait until lunch break to go back to my place. I know that Katya goes to the farmer's market with Constantine on Fridays to sample the local treats. Tryan nervously plays with the strings on his hoodie while I repeatedly tap on the steering wheel, watching a shadow as it dances around the hood of my car. Finally, Katya and Constantine leave the driveway, and we slip out of the car and into the house.

Inside the studio, Tryan maneuvers around the covered paintings, before reaching the window where he closes the curtains.

"Where do we start?" I ask.

"I need all your senses turned off so you can listen," he says, coming back to the door and leaning past me to shut off the light.

He moves so quickly, I don't have time to react. As he reaches across me, I close my eyes and inhale his cologne.

"That's it," Tryan whispers in my ear, tickling my skin. "Focus on the sounds."

I try to ignore his smell and listen, but it's difficult. It reminds me of when we got too close in the forest, when we danced last night, and this morning when he brushed against me by the piano. I ball my hands into fists and get myself under control, forcing myself to concentrate on listening.

At first, all I can hear is my breathing, which starts out fast. As I listen, it settles and eventually gets quiet. I start to think about the voice that called out to me last night. But right now there's nothing except my heartbeat. Only, instead of it staying in a rhythmical pattern, it gets faster, then slower, and repeats. I realize that the sound I'm hearing is not just my heartbeat—there's another.

"Oh!"

"Shhh," Tryan says, putting his hand on my arm. The one heartbeat in the background speeds up slightly. "Follow the sound you hear."

I take a few steps forward, and the faster heartbeat gets louder. I turn instinctively toward the window I saw the shadowed figure the night before. The heartbeat reciprocates each step, getting faster and faster until I reach the window and it stops. I open my eyes, but nothing is there.

"It's gone," I say, reaching out to the curtain.

"Wait," Tryan says. "What do you see?"

I peer around the edges of the window and see a dark shadow

playing at the base of the curtain. At first, it just sits there, then it shoots out, and the sound of the heartbeat enters my ears again. It slips up the wall, behind a draped painting hanging next to the window.

"What was that?" I ask.

"That was a demon," Tryan says, letting go of my arm and running back to turn on the light.

I pull off the linen, and drop it to the floor, observing the painting behind it. Tall trees in the painting open into a clearing in the woods. In the center lies a stone table.

"What do you see?" I ask Tryan.

He stands beside me and looks up at the painting, staring at it for a moment, peering closer to its canvas. Then suddenly, he pushes me back and grabs the linen, throwing it back over the painting.

"Is this the one that was calling to you?" Tryan asks, turning toward me and grabbing my arms.

"No, not exactly," I say.

"This isn't a game, Dacie," Tryan says. "Some demons are worse than others."

"What was it?" I ask.

Tryan walks away, shaking his head, making me feel like a child who just got in trouble for something she didn't know she did.

"What then?" I ask, getting mad. "You're just going to quit."

"This was a stupid idea," he says. "I'm not sure why I thought we should do this."

"You're giving up on me?"

"I didn't say that," he says, looking at me awkwardly. "It's my job to watch out for you; part of that means waiting until you're ready to summon."

"It's not your job to do anything with me," I say, leaning back against the wall and crossing my arms. "You're not my tovaros."

A smile plays at the edge of Tryan's lips. "What makes you think I'm not?"

His words surprise me, and I'm suddenly speechless. Tryan walks over to me and leans on the wall next to me. "How would you know if I was?"

"I expect there would be a sign of some kind."

Tryan laughs aloud and I can feel my face turn red.

"What sort of a sign do you want?" he asks. "Lightning to strike the house?"

I look away. Ridicule is not something I'm in the mood for right now.

"I'm sorry," he says, "but there's no sign. Either we work well together, or we don't. We won't know until you're old enough to summon."

He bumps playfully against my shoulder, but I'm too angry to respond. "I didn't mean to—"

The linen of the painting next to me shoots out into the room, then lies back down. Tryan grabs me by the arm and pulls me on the other side of him.

"What was that?" I ask.

"I don't know," he says, slowly circling the painting on its opposite side. He reaches out toward the linen, and the center of the cloth jumps out again. In one sweep, Tryan pulls it from the painting to the floor. The painting stands still against the wall, and I'm surprised to see it's a mess of colors.

"What's in it?" I ask.

Tryan peers into the painting. "Odd," he says, "I can't see anything."

I look down to the floor next to him and see something drawn on the inside of the linen. It's a simple sketch of a mountain covered in snow. I peer closer and can almost feel a chill pass through the room. Tryan says something to me, but his voice is muffled. The mountain begins to tremble as an avalanche begins down one of its peaks.

"Dacie! No!"

It's too late; before I realize what's happening something begins to rise from the sheet.

"How do I put it back?" I scream to Tryan.

A thick arm reaches out of the bulge and knocks me against the wall. I land on the floor and gasp for air as I try to catch my breath. A large creature crawls out of the linen; its face is scrunched up and scarred, and it's ten times bigger than the imp. Tryan jumps on its back as it stands and it pulls its other arm from the linen, revealing a large ax. A scream escapes my lips before I can get to my feet.

The creature struggles against Tryan, who's trying to choke him from behind. Its thick neck is impossible to get arms around, and instead, it reaches behind and grabs Tryan, throwing him against the wall across the room.

I jump up and scramble toward Tryan's limp body. The creature lets out a loud howl and steps toward me. I grab Tryan by the arm and try to pull him from the room.

"Wake up," I plead.

Tryan's eyes open.

"My arm." He winces in pain. I look down and see it twisted and crooked underneath him.

The creature lets out another howl, then steps toward us, knocking the easels that stand in its path. Looming over us, it lifts up its ax high into the air.

The door to the studio bursts open, and Constantine runs in, holding a sword in his hand. It's the one I always see him polishing in the study. The ax crashes against the sword, but Constantine holds his ground against the enormous creature.

"Get back," Constantine shouts. At first, I think he's talking to us, but then I realize it's meant for the creature. "Get back where you came from, ogre."

The ogre lifts its ax, sweeping it horizontally at Constantine. He jumps up into the air, and the ax flies underneath him. Constantine strikes at the ogre, catching the creature on its arm, and a thin line of blood appears. The ogre lets out another howl.

Katya appears in the doorway with paints in hand. Constantine corners the ogre back toward the linen where it came from. As Katya approaches the pair, she begins to throw paint on the ogre, and it splashes against the sheet. The ogre hollers again as it begins to merge with the painting. Constantine holds it back with his sword, as Katya continues to cover the ogre in paint, and soon it disappears into the drawing.

Constantine turns toward me with his lips pursed, but it's not him I'm worried about. I brace myself as Katya turns around with wild eyes.

"What on earth have you two been up to?" she exclaims.

Tryan goes limp in my arms, and I look down at his ashen face. "Please, help him," I cry.

CHAPTER THIRTEEN

At the hospital, Katya and I sit waiting as Tryan's arm is set in a cast. I look over at my great-aunt, watching as she picks at the dried paint in her nail beds. Her gold rings glisten in the glaring white hospital lights and her many bracelets clang together as she exaggerates each movement. I wish Constantine hadn't stayed behind to clean up the mess. I could sure use some interference here.

"I'm sorry, all right?"

Katya ignores me and keeps cleaning.

"I said, I'm sorry." I enunciate every word.

"Sorry. For. What?" Katya slowly pronounces each word in her accent. "Sorry for wrecking my studio? Sorry for getting Tryan hurt? Or are you sorry for putting everyone in this town at risk with what you almost let free?"

"All of it," I grumble, sitting back into my seat. I cross my arms and look down the hallway.

Katya keeps cleaning her nails.

"You know this isn't my fault," I whisper. "I didn't ask for this life."

"Now you sound like your mother."

"I can see why she ran away from all of you," I say. "Imps and ogres—what's next?"

"Imps?" Katya says, sitting up and staring at me. "What about imps?"

"That happened the other night," I say. "Tryan helped me put it back."

"You're out of control." She shakes her head.

"I have no idea what I'm doing!" I say, a little too loud. People in the waiting area look at us and whisper.

"Come with me." Katya grabs my hand and pulls me toward the vending machines. There I lean against the wall, away from the prying eyes of strangers.

"I get you are mad at me because you have just learned of your ability," she says. "But it is your mother who never told you about your lineage, not me. As for imps and ogres, no more secrets, got it? There are rules for summoners: You are fully responsible for anything you let out, and can be held responsible in court for their wrongdoings if you do not take swift action to get a demon under control, understand?"

"I don't think any court believes in demons."

"Not here." Katya rolls her eyes. "Courts back home in Romania. You will be punished to the extent of the summoner laws."

"What do you mean, 'summoner laws'?" I ask.

"I knew I should have taken you back home." Katya waves her hands in the air. "What can you learn of any importance here? But no, Constantine says, let the girl finish her education. Meh."

"What can happen if a demon gets out of control?"

"If they kill, it's as if you killed," she says, her eyes bearing down on me. "Your only salvation is to capture them and send them back to the other side immediately. Then, and only then, might the courts take mercy on you."

"How are you supposed to keep tabs on all the demons?"

"You pick and choose who you let out," she says. "Then you monitor them. If they break your rules, you send them home."

"How could anyone monitor that ogre?"

"Onri?" Katya says. "He's not so bad. He's a guardian for my studio. Keeps eyes on who should be in there and who shouldn't be."

A doctor flags us over and takes us to see Tryan. We walk down the hallway with the squeaky-clean floor, and I make sure to avoid staring at any of the paintings on the walls. What if the imp did something I'm not aware of? Tryan said it was more dangerous than I realized. *Could I be punished when I didn't even know I was able to summon?*

"Tryan," Katya says as we enter his room, "are you all right?"

"I'll survive," he says, lifting up his arm, now wrapped in gauze. I walk over to the other side of his bed and see his fingers peeking out from the end, all black and blue from the attack. I reach out and run my finger along his arm.

"I forgot my bag," Katya says, leaving the room.

"Are you really okay?"

"I'm fine," Tryan says. "Are you okay? You look a little like you've seen a ghost."

"No," I say, "just an ogre."

I look up at his face and see that a smile plays at the edge of his mouth. He laughs aloud and then winces.

"Sorry," he says, "broken rib. Some tovaros I am. Maybe we aren't such a great match."

I bite back tears. *Don't cry, Dacie.* But this is all overwhelming. The imp was weird enough, but now ogres and demons in paintings. *If Tryan isn't a match for me, who is?* I wish I were back in California. I turn away, and my long brown hair falls across my face.

"Hey," he says, reaching across and grabbing my hand, "are you sure you're okay? It'll be fine, you know. You did okay; you're just new to all of this."

"How am I supposed to get used to this?"

"Eventually it'll be like second nature," Tryan says, squeezing my hand. I look back at him, and he's smiling. I let go of his hand, knowing it must hurt him to reach across like that. I walk around the bed and sit in a chair on his good side.

"So what now?" I ask.

"We go back to school," he says. "I heal, life goes on."

"Like nothing happened?"

Tryan nods. "When I'm better we'll start training together if you want."

"Really," I say, perking up. Then my excitement falls. "But you'll be out of commission for a couple of months."

"Hopefully I heal faster than that," Tryan says, shifting in his bed. "Then I can teach you a few things about summoning."

"Such as the laws?"

"That's a good place to start," Katya says from the doorway. "We better give this man his rest now, Daciana."

I look back at Tryan, and he smiles. "I'll come see you tomorrow."

"Deal."

As we walk down the hall, I ponder the glimmer of hope Tryan has given me toward a future of summoning. Maybe life won't be so bad with this ability. But what if he isn't my tovaros?

"When did you and Constantine meet?"

"Oh," Katya says, "so long ago I can't even remember."

"Obviously, he's your tovaros," I say. "You must have learned about summoning together?"

"Back home one learns about summoning from birth," Katya says. "My mother summoned demons while I was a babe tied to her back. I always knew it was what I would grow up to do. Everyone back home knows this. We accept it."

"Mom obviously didn't."

"Your mother was different," Katya explains. "She had her own inner demons she dealt with."

"So you knew you needed a tovaros before you met Constantine?"

"Yes," Katya says, "I suppose it makes the matching less troublesome. Back home everyone is either a tovaros or a summoner. You all hang out together until you find your compatibility."

"Did you date many before Constantine?"

"Oh, Daciana." Katya chuckles. "It isn't like that. A tovaros is a great friend, yes. Soul mates, yes. But not necessarily a love connection. That just happens with some."

"So you and Constantine never—"

"Long ago." Katya smiles with a twinkle in her eye.

I can't help but smile.

"Do not place all your hope in this tovaros," Katya warns. "A summoner must be strong, above all. We will start your training immediately."

"Really?"

"It is time you learn where you come from."

I follow Katya, about to burst in anticipation of beginning my training. I'm so caught up in the moment that I duck and scream when a flash of bright light zips past me.

"What's the matter?"

I shrug. Katya obviously didn't see what I did. When she turns away, I check behind me, and see that the doors to the hospital chapel are wide open. A young boy pokes his head out the doors and stares at me with wide eyes. I look away and push the thoughts of the white light out of my head as I focus on what I'm about to learn.

CHAPTER
FOURTEEN

When we get inside, Katya disappears for a moment, then returns with a large brown book she passes to me. I run my fingers across the wrinkled old leather, scripted with the words *"Book of Summoning"* across its cover. Underneath the words is a carving of scales, which sit even on both sides, and underneath that reads: *Ours is not for judgment, but for balance.*

"Is this for me?" I ask, turning the book over in my hands. I sit down on the couch and flip it open.

"It is," Katya says, sitting next to me. "This book has all of the skills a summoner needs to learn. I'd like you to start with chapter three."

I excitedly flip through the book until I reach *Chapter Three: The Laws of Summoning*:

Law One: A summoner is responsible for all creatures it lets through from the netherworld.

Law Two: If a creature carries out immoral or unscrupulous acts, a summoner must instantly send it back to the netherworld, or be held fully responsible for the acts carried out by the creatures in its care.

Law Three: The Summoner Guild determines all forms of punishment, which will be voted on by the members of the guild. In the event of a stalemate, the tovaros of the summoner will be the deciding vote. If a tovaros does not yet exist, then this swing vote will fall to the Tovaros High Senate.

"That's it?" I say. "Three laws? I thought it would be a little more laborious than this."

"Stick out your hand," Katya says.

I look at her, confused, as I stick out my hand. She grabs it and flips it over palm up, without taking her eyes off mine.

"Do you solemnly swear to uphold the three laws of summoning, so hope you die?"

I start to laugh, but Katya shakes her head at me and tightens her grip on my hand. I wince in pain and firmly stare back at her.

"Fine," I say. "Yes."

"Let it be heard you have sworn to follow the three laws," Katya says, and with one swift movement, she pulls out a dagger from behind her back and pierces my palm.

"Ahh!" I scream as a burning pain sears across my flesh. "What the hell did you do?"

I pull my hand back close to me and close my fingers around my wound. I can feel my warm blood gathering in my palm, as it slips through my fingers, dripping onto the page of the book.

"You have now signed in your blood," Katya says. "You are officially bound by those rules forever."

I snatch my hand back and turn on my heels, running up to my bedroom.

"Daciana!" she calls after me, but I slam my door shut after grabbing a towel from the linen closet.

What a bag. Tears sting my eyes as I bandage up my hand the best I can while sitting at my desk. The open page of the book has drops of my blood on it, which I try to wipe away. The paper remains stained and in the light of my desk lamp, other marks stain the page. How many summoners came before me?

I flip through the pages of the book, going back to the beginning. It starts with a history section, which I idly flip through, pausing at some gruesome drawings from times in the past of plague and illness, when apparently demons ravaged humankind.

The next chapter discusses the importance of the balance of good and evil. *One cannot exist without the other.* It briefly speaks of how, without demons, the power of seraphs would blind and tear apart humankind, while without good, demons would ravage and destroy all living things. *The importance of the demon summoner is to maintain this balance and ensure the lives of humankind are preserved.*

I sit back in my chair and think those words over. Am I responsible for humanity? A sickening feeling begins to push against my chest, and sweat breaks out on my forehead. What am I supposed to do? I don't even know how to control the little powers I have now. I lean over and put my head in my hands. I wish Tryan were available to talk to—I really need a friend.

A quiet knock sounds at my door, and I jump up from my chair. "Leave me alone, Katya." I shout, wiping a tear from my eye.

"It's not Katya," Constantine says from the other side. "Though she did ask me to check on you."

"Come in." I sigh, sitting back down.

Constantine enters my room slowly, looking around at everything before finally settling his eyes on me in the chair. He's carrying a first aid kit.

"Let me see your hand," he says, reaching out to me.

I reluctantly hold out my hand, encircled with the blood-soaked towel.

"Tsk, tsk," Constantine says, unwrapping my makeshift bandage. He clicks open the first aid kit and begins to clean my wound. "Doesn't look like you will need stitches."

"Are you a doctor?" I ask, quickly wishing it hadn't come out so sharp.

"Once," he says, still focusing on my wound. "But that was another life."

"A gardener and a doctor?" I ask. "What an odd combination."

"You're missing town drunk and lost soul," he says.

I start to laugh, then realize Constantine is serious. "What do you mean?"

"That was long ago, Daciana." Constantine sighs, starting to bandage my wound with clean gauze and tape. "Before Katya found me."

"So all of our lives would've been lost without her," I say, looking away.

"Not so. I had lost my medical license and was living in the streets of Romania. Katya saved me, gave me purpose again. Now, I remember six months ago, traveling to California, and finding a quiet and scared little girl there. Look at you now, strong and confident. You did it on your own, but Katya was the one to come and find you."

I shrug, pulling my bandaged hand away from Constantine and looking back to the book on the desk. He leans over my shoulder and glances at my reading.

"I always liked chapter five." Constantine smiles, then walks to the door. "Lots of useful information there."

As soon as he closes the door, I flip to chapter five. *Anthology of Demons: Strengths and Weaknesses.* I smile to myself and start reading.

I can't wait for visiting hours to begin the next day. I was up most of the night before, reading chapter five, making mental notes on imps and ogres. My choices to overtake them pretty much consist of spells and poisons, which I know nothing about and would most likely wind up hurting myself if I tried it on my own. Aside from those two forms of demons, I wasn't sure what else I could expect to run into in Katya's studio.

The hospital is filled with people, and plagued by shadows skimming about in every corner. Chapter One told me that demons preyed on the weak; a hospital must be like a buffet for them.

When I enter Tryan's room, he's sound asleep. I pull up a chair next to his bed, and wait for him to wake up. His features are softer when he sleeps: his jaw more relaxed and his lips are fuller. His chest rises and falls with each breath, and my thoughts flicker to how it looked when I first saw him in the forest. I can feel the pull between us, being this close to him.

The rhythm of Tryan's breathing makes my eyelids feel heavy. My lack of sleep from the night before is catching up to me. I notice a dark shadow extend out from the corner of his room to the door. *Not now*, I think as I lay my head on the bed and close my eyes.

I startle at the touch of a hand running through my hair. Mom? A hospital room comes into focus. I remember where I am, and that my mom isn't around anymore. My heart clenches. Sometimes clarity isn't wanted.

"Sorry," Tryan says. "Did I wake you up?"

"No," I say, awkwardly sitting up and running my hands through my hair, trying to shake the sensation of my mother away from me. "I didn't mean to fall asleep."

"That's okay," he says. "I'm glad you came. It looks like I'm getting out tomorrow."

"What? I thought your arm was broken."

"So did the doctor," he says, holding up his bandaged arm. "But it's just a bad sprain."

"Did they do x-rays?"

"I was scheduled for a cast today," he says, "but I told them how much better it felt. They checked it over, x-rayed again, and couldn't believe it; must have been a blip on the original pic."

"What about your ribs?"

"Much better."

I look at Tryan suspiciously. A smile plays around his lips, and I can't shake the feeling that he's hiding something from me. "So you seriously get to go home tomorrow."

"Yes," he says. "I thought we could hang out tomorrow night. Maybe go to a movie or something."

"Really?" I roll my eyes. "Isn't that pretty standard. Isn't there anything special that summoners and their tovaros's do?"

He chuckles quietly. "Listen. We're lucky neither of us was seriously hurt yesterday. I don't know what I would have done if something happened to you." Tryan's eyes grow dark. "We need to have a little fun together that doesn't involve imps or ogres, right?"

He leans forward and grabs my hand with his. I'm instantly embarrassed at how nervous I feel, but the pull is stronger when we touch and I feel myself leaning toward him. A nurse walks in and instantly blushes when she sees us. I instantly let go, and drop back in my chair.

"Sorry," she says. "I need to wheel this guy off to one more set of x-rays."

I look outside and see the evening darkness begin to set in. "I better get home," I say, disappointed in the little time we have.

"Pick me up at noon tomorrow?" he asks.

"Absolutely," I say, smiling as disappointment is replaced with possibilities.

As I leave the hospital I wonder about Tryan's arm; it was bent in such a crooked direction when he passed out in the studio, I can't believe it isn't broken. I still can't shake the feeling he's hiding something from me.

As I reach the chapel doors, the same young boy from yesterday, jumps out in front of me. He can't be more than twelve years old. I step to the side to avoid him, but he steps in front of me again.

"Hey," I say. "I'm in a hurry."

"I know what you are," he says, staring up at me with the same wide eyes as yesterday. A shiver jolts through me like a knife in my chest.

"Eli," a man's voice says from the chapel. A robed priest appears in the doorway; his eyes scan me, then turn to the boy. "Back inside."

The boy walks back to the chapel, watching me as the man closes the doors between us. A shiver runs down my spine this time, causing goosebumps to form on my arms. I hurry out of the hospital, not wanting to know what the boy meant.

CHAPTER FIFTEEN

"Katya says you have to come for lunch," I say as I pick Tryan up the next day from the hospital.

"Maybe she likes me after all." He winks.

"I think it's a guilt lunch," I laugh. "*Sorry my guardian ogre attacked you, here have some sandwiches.*"

Tryan laughs aloud before turning serious. "Will we still hang out later?" he asks. "Alone?"

"Yes." I nod.

As I wheel him out of the hospital, I hesitate at the chapel doors. They are wide open again, but this time no one is inside. My mystery boy will have to remain that way, I guess.

"What are you looking for?" Tryan asks, peering toward the chapel.

"Nothing." I hurriedly push him away.

"We're glad to see you healed so quickly," Katya says, raising an eyebrow. "No sign of a break in the second set of x-rays, hmm?"

"No, ma'am," Tryan says, chewing his sandwich.

"Practically a miracle," Katya says. A smile is plastered on her face, but it looks more suspicious than genuine. "Constantine heals like that as well."

"Not before I met you." He winks at Katya.

They exchange a knowing look, making me smile at their connection. I can't help it—I enjoy watching them together. Thoughts of my mother drift into my mind; had she found her tovaros, would she have had happiness like this?

"So, Tryan," Katya says, "I did some research, seeing as we are going to be seeing more of you. We have to look out for Daciana, you know."

Tryan suddenly looks pale and puts his food down.

"It's interesting," she says. "Orphaned at thirteen. Star student up until last year, when you fall off the grid. That is, until a few months ago."

I frown at Katya. This hardly seems the time to grill a newcomer. It's not like he's my boyfriend or anything. I look over at Tryan, whose face has paled.

"Are you okay?" I ask.

"I—don't feel so good," Tryan says, rubbing his hands against one another. "I must have eaten too fast."

Katya nods. "Take him home, Daciana. He's been through a lot."

"I'll walk," he says, getting up. "I think the air will be good for me."

"Don't be silly." I stand and grab our plates. "It's the least I owe you for getting you into this mess."

"Please," Katya adds, "don't hesitate to come back as soon as you're feeling better. I'd love to learn more about your family, friends, and acquaintances."

Tryan almost knocks his chair over as he leaves the table. I glance back at Katya in confusion, but she only shrugs and continues with her lunch. Once we're in the car, Tryan gives me directions to his place. He lives on the other side of the woods, behind our house. I'm excited to have some time alone, but the air is thick with silence. I try to make small talk a few times, but Tryan seems preoccupied with the scenery out the window. Finally, the silence breaks.

"When do you get some hands-on training?" he asks, resting his hands next to mine.

"Soon I hope. I wonder what will be first? Weapons training? Or will I get to summon something new?"

"Nice to see you're not so down about the whole summoning-thing anymore." He pats my hand, sending a burst of excitement up my arm into my chest.

"Now I have Katya to help me," I say, "and you."

"Dacie—"

"It's just nice to focus on something new," I say, stopping him from raining on my parade. "I've spent the last six months in the shadow of what happened to my mom."

"Right." He sighs. "I just want you to know there'll be a lot of reading."

"Reading?"

"Yes," he says. "It's not all fun and games. I don't envy you one bit. I'd take a broken arm over that stuff any day."

I laugh as I pull up to his house. Its windows are dark, and the lawn looks unkempt. Thoughts of Katya's comments come up: *Orphaned at thirteen.* Whom does he live with now? "Do you want me to come in?" I ask. "It doesn't look like anyone's home."

"I'm good," he says, still holding my hand and staring at me.

"What?" Nervous laughter escapes my lips, but Tryan doesn't break a smile. His intensity makes me nervous.

"You know when we saw that ogre?"

"Yeah?"

"Well, it was pretty cool you didn't run away," he says. "Most girls would, you know."

"Not summoners, I suppose."

"No, definitely not." He laughs, leaning his head back. "You're different than them too, though. Maybe it's because you didn't grow up knowing about all of this life."

"So I'm not even normal in summoner terms? I'm doomed to be weird."

Tryan looks over at me, staring at my face. He pushes a lock of hair away from my face. "You're far from weird."

A shiver runs down my back as I move toward him. He leans in and reaches behind me, grabbing his bag from the backseat. "See you at school tomorrow." He flashes me a smile as he gets out of the car.

I sit there in shock at what didn't happen before I manage to speak. "What about tonight?"

"Oh, right," he says. "I'll call if I'm feeling better."

My heart drops. He disappears around the back of the car, then reappears at my window.

"Oh, and Dacie?"

I turn toward him and force a smile.

"No matter what you hear, just try to form your own opinions of me? Okay?"

He leans forward and kisses my cheek, leaving me more confused than I was seconds earlier. I watch him run around to the back of his house, leaving me behind. I force myself to focus on the positive side—he did just get out of the hospital.

"You're far from weird," rings in my ears as I turn the car around and go home.

CHAPTER SIXTEEN

The next day at school, I look for Tryan everywhere. His desk is empty in Art, and I anxiously get through class, hoping to run into him on break, but he's nowhere. Brennan tries to get my attention, but I ignore him. I'm on a mission.

I remember Tryan's house last night—dark and unkempt—and make a plan. If I don't see Tryan by lunch, I'll drive over to his place. He could be lying sick, all alone, and no one would know.

I ask to be excused halfway through class. I'm too distracted to focus on drawing, and I want to try to call Tryan again. But when I get to my locker my phone is dead. Oh, man. I forgot to charge it. There are too many things going on right now. I turn to go back to class, but see Miss Nelson watching me from the other end of the hallway.

"Everything okay?" she asks, waving me over.

"Fine. Just checking on a friend."

"A friend? Or something more?" she asks, offering a smile. "We're talking about Tryan, right?"

I nod.

"Have you known him long?" she asks.

"I just moved here."

"So he's not a family friend?"

I narrow my stare at her. These are nosy questions, even for a counselor.

She laughs. "I'm sorry. I meant, what do you know about him? It's hard being in a new place, and meeting new people. Sometimes we put our trust too readily in something that seems comfortable and then we're open to disappointment."

"It's not like that," I say, backing away.

"Wait," she says, reaching out. "I'm sorry. I'm going about this the wrong way. I've been worried about Tryan since he started here. He hasn't made friends easily. I'm glad he met you."

A small bit of relief lifts my apprehension. "We're just friends. He missed school this morning. I was worried about him."

"Then you're a good friend," she says. "I'll go check on him if that makes you feel better."

I nod. It does.

The bell rings, and I leave Miss Nelson with her promise, making my way to History. There, the instructor drones on about founding families, as we finally move through the eighteenth century. But I'm too distracted to pay attention. Outside the turning leaves shift in the breeze and the sun comes through the fall skies, tricking the senses into thinking it's still summer.

"Miss Cantar?" The teacher clears his throat. "Did you hear me?"

I turn away from the windows as my class breaks out into snickers. "Sorry? What?"

"What do you know about your family history?" he asks.

My eyes grow wide, and my throat goes dry. I thought we were talking about founding families? What does this have to do with mine?

"Tell us about the Cantars," he prompts, looking impatient.

Umm, I'm sure he doesn't want to know what I've recently learned. I doubt it's written in any of his history books. "I don't know anything." I shrug. "My mother never spoke about her family."

The teacher frowns. "Well then, your paper for next week can be to tell us a little something about your family. I'll keep it short to make it easy: 1,000 words on the Cantars, okay?"

My mouth drops open. Is he serious? What can I tell them? The Cantars come from a long line of demon summoners to keep good and evil in balance so the rest of you can live normal lives. Hey, maybe I'll even bring a painting for a demonstration. A smile crawls across my face at the idea of Chantal meeting an Ifrit.

The bell rings, and I jump up from my desk, but before I can leave, the intercom crackles. "Daciana Cantar, please report to the office."

Oh no? Did something happen to Tryan?

"Miss Cantar?" the assistant says, raising an eyebrow. I nod and stand.

It's a new girl this time, younger than the regular. She must be a sub. Her hair is parted down the middle into two braids, making her look even younger. Does she know what news the principal has for me? Maybe if I interrogated her a little —

"The principal will see you now."

In the office, Principal Smyth is on one side of the desk, and Brennan on the other. What does this have to do with Tryan? The principal welcomes me. "Daciana, please have a seat."

Brennan looks away sheepishly as I sit next to him. His leg is bouncing up and down, like he's nervous or something. What could this be about? Does he know something about Tryan?

"I'm glad things are getting better." She smiles at me.

"Are they?" I ask, looking at Brennan, but he's still avoiding my eyes. I notice his finger has started tapping on his binder.

"To the point." Principal Smyth clears her throat. "I must admit, I do have an agenda for bringing you here. I'm electing a yearbook committee and Brennan tells me you're quite the artist."

"Yearbook?" I'm confused.

"Yes, Brennan is in charge of the yearbook, and frankly, we were hoping you might agree to help out with some sketches. I'd like to make it more personal and fun for the students, using original artwork rather than just some random clipart."

I relax. "Is that all?"

The principal raises an eyebrow. "Are you in?"

They both look at me with an excitement I have to force onto my face. It actually sounds fun, drawing for the yearbook, an honor. Right now, all I can think of is Tryan, so I give them what they want in return for my escape.

"Absolutely."

"Awesome," Brennan says from beside me. I don't turn to look at him. Instead, I stare forward at the principal.

"Can I go?"

She nods. "Don't let me keep you from class."

I hurry out of the office, glancing at Miss Nelson's office door in the next room. Closed. Good. At least she won't head me off at the exit. I sneak down the hallway, but before I get far, Brennan interrupts me.

"Dacie, wait up!"

"Can't. I'm in a hurry."

"I just wanted to say I think this will be fun—"

The door is right in front of me; it's now or never. I push it open, and the bright sun blinds me for a moment.

"But you'll miss next period," he says.

I glance back only once and see him standing by the rear door, looking like a lost kid. Guilt flutters in my stomach for a second, but then it dissolves somewhere in my gut. I've other boys to worry about, Brennan. Sorry.

I wave from the car as I drive past, on my way out of the school parking lot. All the way to Tryan's house, I keep picturing him lying injured, all alone. I should've stayed with him until someone else got there last night.

When I get to Tryan's house, I pull up on the wrong side of the street and run to the door. When I knock, it slowly creaks open. *Why isn't it locked?* I push it open all the way and peer inside. The smell of stale chips and sweat makes my nose wrinkle.

"Tryan? Are you here?"

Silence.

I step carefully into the room. "Tryan!"

Nothing.

The living room looks like someone's been living in it. Bedding is on the couch and clothes are piled in the corner. But that's not what concerns me; a lamp and end table are knocked over, and the coffee table is all busted up. It looks like someone got into a fight in here.

"Tryan!" I call out, running down the hall into the bedrooms. They're empty. I run back to the living room and pause in the kitchen. A single cup and plate rest on the counter. I have a suspicious feeling creeping in the back of my mind; I throw open the cupboard doors and check the fridge. Nothing. *Tryan lives alone?*

My heart races and my breath starts coming out in short bursts. *What's going on? Where's Tryan?* I put the lamp and table upright, then stand staring at the room, feeling lost.

Katya will know what to do. I run outside and get back into my car, but when I put the keys in the ignition, it won't start.

"Ahh!" I slam my hands on the steering wheel. I grab my bag from the passenger seat and run toward the woods.

In the woods, the sun peeks through the dense trees, casting rays of sun on the path in front of me. I run as fast as I can, as if the quicker I get home, the quicker this will all be over. When the house comes into view, I slow down. My lungs feel ready to explode; I don't even run like this in gym class.

I stop to catch my breath, and hear footsteps running behind me. I jerk my head back to look, but the sound stops and nothing is there. I stand frozen, feeling my skin vibrating from the adrenaline, when I hear a rustling from my left. I sharply turn and peer toward the noise, but again nothing's there.

My legs feel like they're glued to the path, but I force them to move, when suddenly a doe jumps out from the trees and runs across the path. I scream aloud, then start laughing to myself. *A deer!* I'm ridiculous.

I walk toward the house, my legs trembling like Jell-O. I hear something move, and look back expecting another deer, but instead there is a dark figure. It has the same tall, lean shape as the one behind the window in Katya's studio, the night of the storm. I don't wait to hear it call my name; I turn and break out into a full run.

This time I don't stop until I reach the back door. I pound on the glass of the patio doors as I fumble with the handle. I look back to the trees on the other side of the yard, but can't see anything pursuing me. *Maybe it was my imagination.* Suddenly the door breaks free, and I fall into Katya's arms.

"Oh, my dear girl!" Katya exclaims. "Whatever is the matter? You look like you've seen death incarnate."

"I—woods—deer—Tryan—gone," I stammer between breaths.

Katya sits me at the table and pours a glass of water.

I sip the water as best I can, dribbling all over my chin as I shake from my exhaustion. I set the glass down and take a few deep breaths.

"There," Katya says, sitting across from me and grabbing my hands. "Now, tell me what happened."

"Tryan wasn't at school this morning," I explain, still gasping for air. "I went to his house. It looks like there was a struggle, so I ran here, and—"

Katya interrupts me. "Tryan stopped by this morning. He left you this note."

I reach out for the paper, forgetting all about the dark figure in the woods. The note shakes in my hand as I unfold it and read its words:

Dacie–
Had to go back home for the weekend. Be back soon.
—Tryan

That's it? He went home. I set the note down and look up at my great-aunt, shaking my head.

"It doesn't make sense," I say. "I saw the knocked over and broken furniture. Are you sure he was alone?"

"I didn't really look," she says. "Where's your car?"

"It wouldn't start," I say. "I left it at Tryan's."

"I'll send Constantine for your car," Katya says, standing up. "He can check Tryan's house while he's there."

A visual of the dark figure in the woods flashes in my thoughts. "Tell him to take his sword."

CHAPTER SEVENTEEN

Katya watches me suspiciously as I pace the front room, waiting for Constantine to return with my car. I keep looking out the curtains, watching for any sign of him, but really, I just hope that he comes back with news about Tryan. I can feel beads of sweat trickling down my back from the stress.

"Did Tryan say anything to you?" she asks. "You know, about you and him?"

"No," I say uncomfortably. "What do you mean?"

"Never mind." She sighs, fidgeting in her chair with her hands in her lap.

I pause and stare at her for a moment. Katya is always so sure of herself; she never seems nervous.

"What's wrong?"

"Hmm?" she says, looking up at me. "Oh, nothing."

"Katya." I walk to her chair. "What is it? Do you know something about Tryan you're not telling me?"

"Not exactly."

My heart races in my chest. "Tell me."

"I believe Tryan is your tovaros," she says as she stares directly at me.

I start to laugh aloud, but she purses her lips tighter and continues to stare me down.

"How can you tell that?" I ask. "We've barely spent time together. Plus, look what happened with your ogre."

"The incident with the ogre is exactly what I'm talking about," she says. "Didn't you think it was suspicious how quickly he healed from his injuries?"

"It was a sprain—"

"A boy like Tryan would not pass out from a sprain," she says. "He healed quickly, as a tovaros linked with his summoner should; the bond gives you immortal attributes."

"Immortality?" I stammer. "You mean, like, live forever?"

"In a sense." She nods. "Truly just a little longer than most. Together you will heal faster and be stronger. Your senses will heighten, and your abilities multiply. The bond between tovaros and summoner is indestructible."

I turn back to the window as my mind races with this new information. *Is Tryan really my tovaros?* The thought of being tied to him forever makes me blush. Is he my soul-mate? It would explain why I always feel a pull toward him.

"Why would that make him want to leave then?" I ask. "He couldn't stand the idea of being with me?"

Katya rolls her eyes. "I'm afraid it has to do with his past. Has he mentioned anything?"

Tryan's last words to me: *"No matter what you hear, just try to make your own opinions of me."* Was he talking about his past? I shake my head, and she only sighs. How bad could it be?

I jump as Constantine comes through the door. He looks calm, which is good—or does he look somber? *I can't stand this.*

"Did you find anything out about Tryan?" I ask.

"No." Constantine's eyes soften, and my heart drops.

"What did you find out?" Katya asks.

"He was summoned home by the Senate," Constantine says. "Don't worry; he's all right."

"What does that mean?" I ask, looking at Katya. Her features have relaxed, but the unknown is still unsettling.

"It means he has to provide a report in front of the Senate and then he's allowed to come back," Constantine says. "That's all, just standard protocol."

I can't help but let a smile crawl across my face. I look away as it gets bigger. "I'm going to go read some more." I turn toward the stairs.

"Okay, Daciana," Katya says. "And I think it's time you begin your next stage of training tomorrow."

"What's that?" I ask, turning back from the stairs.

"Self-defense." Constantine smiles back.

My dreams are calmer than usual. Visions of Tryan skip around at the edges, keeping the dark shadows at bay, but my frustration increases as he's never close enough to be within my reach. Each time I get a little closer though, and just as I can feel the heat of his body on my fingertips, I'm pulled from the depths of sleep into reality.

A quiet knock wakes me up.

"What is it?" I lift my heavy head from the pillow. Did I sleep at all?

"It's time," Constantine says, standing in my bedroom doorway with his arms crossed and a serious look on his face.

"Time for sleep," I grumble, rolling over in bed and putting my pillow over my face.

His muffled voice reaches my ears. "Time for training."

"What is the actual time?" I ask, sitting up in bed.

"Five o'clock in the morning." A smile plays at the edge of his mouth.

"What!"

I look over to my desk, where I spent the remainder of the day before and a good part of the night memorizing demons and their strengths and weaknesses.

"I don't do this early," I advise Constantine.

"Meet me in the den in five minutes," he says, leaving my bedroom door open.

I throw my pillow where he stood in a lame attempt to resist and grumble to myself as I drag my butt out of bed. A change of clothes, a ponytail, and one brushed set of teeth later, I arrive in Constantine's den before him, with one minute to spare.

I glance up at his sword, hanging above the mantle of the fireplace. It still seems odd that Constantine used that to fend off an ogre in this house. My great-aunt's quiet gardener has proven to be much more than I ever imagined.

I walk over to the bar, which holds various types of coffee and tea from all over the world. I pick up a red container next to me with a label written in a language I've never seen before.

"That's a Syrian tea." Constantine's voice startles me.

I spin around to face him.

"Tea is not just for the British," he says. "The Middle East, Asians, South Americans, and many more make it an important part of their culture."

"You know a lot about the world," I say, putting the container back on the bar. "Funny, not a drop of alcohol in here."

"Why is that funny?" he asks. "I thought you of all people would be grateful."

"I just meant because it's a bar … " Suddenly, I see Constantine in a different light. He's more opinionated than the quiet gardener I had grown to know.

"Come with me," he says, walking to the bookshelf next to the desk.

"Where are we going?"

He reaches up to the fifth shelf and counts in seven books. "There we go." Constantine turns to me and winks. "Sun Tzu's, *The Art of War*." As he pulls out the book, I hear a click. The bookshelf trembles then pushes inwards, revealing a narrow staircase that goes down.

"After you." He motions for me to pass through.

As I descend the stone steps, my footsteps echo into the darkness below. Shadows whip around my feet, feeding on both my fear and the coldness of the unknown. When I step off the last step the room lights up, and the shadows scurry away into the corners.

The floor is covered in mats, and the walls are lined with various weapons. The room has a dank smell to it: a mix of mud and sweat. I wrinkle up my nose as I walk across the mats.

"Self-defense is the most important skill a summoner can learn," Constantine says as he enters the room behind me. "Sure, you can study all the demons along with their weaknesses and strengths, and of course, you will learn to master your skill as a painter so you can trap a demon effectively, but if you can't protect yourself from an attack, all the above is useless to you."

"I thought a summoner and their tovaros are practically immortal when together."

Constantine raises an eyebrow. "You would risk your life on *practically?*"

I frown and shake my head.

"Then let's get started," he says.

Constantine walks around me, and as he passes my peripheral vision, the hair on the back of my neck rises. Suddenly, a sharp pain rips across my back, and I find myself on my knees, reeling from the blow.

"What the hell was that?" I cry out in a strained voice, flailing on the floor, trying to reach my back.

"Get up," Constantine says.

I slowly push myself to my feet on shaky legs, and spin around to face him. He still has that stupid smile on his face, but I can only glare back now.

"A summoner must always be aware," he says. "Trust no one. A demon can possess your closest friend at any time."

A shiver runs down my back. Any time? "How can you tell when someone's possessed?"

"They look different, like the shadows have settled just under their skin—sometimes it ripples a little. Then there are the eyes; you can always see it in their eyes."

The same shiver returns, this time breaking out in a cool sweat across the back of my neck. Possession? This is much more than just some imps running around. What kind of demons possess people—and why?

I want to ask more questions, but Constantine circles me. This time I turn, not letting him out of my sight. My heartbeat bangs against my chest, and my breath comes out in short bursts as my adrenaline rises. My fingertips feel like they're going to explode and my legs are still shaking.

Constantine shoots toward me and before I can react, he's knocked my legs out from under me. I lie on my back, gasping for air, as I stare up at the ceiling. A large circle is painted there, covered in symbols I've seen in the *Book of Summoning*.

Constantine appears in my view, holding a hand out to me. I grab it, barely able to hold on as he helps me up. My knees ache, and my back hurts. I feel like we've been doing this forever and we've only just begun.

"A summoner must always be able to read their opponent so that they can guess the next move before it happens," he says, stepping back from me. "Focus, Daciana."

I catch my breath and crouch lower as I watch Constantine. I can feel frustration burning inside me as it reaches down through my limbs, filling my senses with electricity. I watch Constantine as he moves around me, his fingers twitching, his jaw muscles clenching and unclenching. His arm muscle changes slightly, and I jump back just as the arm moves toward me. A look of surprise crosses his face, followed by approval.

"Very good, Daciana," he says. "You learn fast."

After a few more minutes of parrying, Constantine grabs two poles from the wall, throwing one at me. "Let's see how you do with a little more in the mix."

He swipes at my feet, and I jump, but not fast enough. The pole hits my ankle, shooting pain up my leg. "Argh," I cry out as I stumble. Constantine swipes at me again, knocking me onto my back, yet again.

"A demon will not allow you time to recover in a moment of weakness—" he begins.

"I get it," I mutter. "A summoner must fight through the pain."

Constantine nods.

It might be an hour or three that passes by, but all I know is when we finish, Tryan is no longer haunting my thoughts. Just the pain in my body remains. I haul myself out of the basement.

"How was practice?" Katya calls from the kitchen, as I pass through the hallway to the staircase.

"Hmpf," I groan.

I shuffle to the bathroom and start a hot bath. As I peel my clothes off, the mirror shows me that dark bruises cover the majority of my skin. I manage to get myself into the tub, where I soak my aching muscles. Damn you, Constantine. *A summoner must look like a beat up piece of meat*—you forgot that one.

I nod off in the tub from exhaustion, then wake up to my stomach grumbling. The water in the tub is cold. *How long have I been in here?* I shiver as I crawl out.

In my bedroom are a sandwich, glass of water, and ibuprofen. I smile, wondering which of my guardians left this for me. As I bite into the sandwich, I pull up my computer. There are two new emails in my inbox. A thought of Tryan flutters in my stomach and I excitedly click on the link, but my enthusiasm crashes as soon as I see both emails are from Brennan.

```
Dacie,
Attached are some yearbook pages that
need sketches. Let me know if you have
any questions.
Brennan
```

The second email arrived an hour later, and it reads:

Dacie,

Just checking if you got my first email.

Brennan

I roll my eyes and close the emails. Brennan's persistent enthusiasm gnaws on the border of irritating.

I put on clean clothes and crawl into bed for a quick nap. If Katya or Constantine needs me, they know where to find me. It doesn't take long for sleep to consume me.

CHAPTER EIGHTEEN

I fill the rest of my weekend with more reading and self-defense classes. Between chapters, I proudly take down Constantine once. He's quick to remind me I'm there to learn how to defend—not attack. It makes me smile.

On Monday morning, I look over my skin, as I get dressed. The bruises are vibrant across my pale skin, like a watercolor painting across a blanket of new snow. The marks are still tender, making me wince as I put my backpack on before going downstairs. On my way out of the house, I grab an apple and quickly run to my car. I'm excited to get to school. Even though I've been busy with training, I didn't forget that Tryan would be back today.

But it's not Tryan I see at my locker. It's Brennan. He excitedly waves to me as I walk inside the school. "Did you get my email?" he asks, when I get closer. "I waited all weekend to hear back from you."

Email? Last time I checked the running total was fifteen. I stopped opening them after the first five. "I did," I say, looking past Brennan, trying to spot Tryan anywhere. The only familiar face I see is Chantal, who glares at me. I turn back to my locker, without directly looking at Brennan. "Sorry, I was busy with homework."

"All weekend?" he says doubtfully.

"Special project." I slam my door shut and turn away. "Catch you later."

As I pass by, I ignore Chantal. Maybe she'll finally get the hint that I'm not her competition. There's only one person I'm interested in at this school, and it's not for romantic purposes. It's only because he has answers that can help me understand my new role.

I don't see Tryan in the hallways or any of my classes throughout the morning. The unknown makes me anxious. Finally, lunch arrives, but by the time I get to the cafeteria, it's packed. I scan the crowd, but the only person looking my way is Brennan, waving at me like an idiot. I nod back, but take my lunch outside to eat alone.

The sun beams down on me, making me sweat as I try to eat my lunch. It's hotter out today than I expected it to be for late fall. But the heat is second to my much larger concern. *Where could Tryan be?* Maybe things didn't go well with the Senate. Will he never be allowed to come back?

The bell rings, and I toss the rest of my lunch in the garbage, before making my way back to my locker. *Great.* Chantal is there waiting for me with her arms crossed. I maintain eye contact, before opening my locker door in front of her face.

"Excuse me," she says with a snotty tone.

"What?" I ask from behind my door.

"What's your problem?" she says, pulling my locker door open further so she can see me. "You're being a *bag* lately."

"I am?" I ask, grabbing my Drama binder and slamming my locker door. "You haven't been kind to me *once* since I met you."

She looks startled and steps back. "I'm not here about me. It's not nice how you ignore Brennan. He's been *so* nice to you."

"You of all people should be glad I'm ignoring Brennan." I brush past her, to make my way to my next class.

Chantal reaches out and grabs my arm, coming right down on a tender spot where Constantine whacked me with a bamboo pole, after we stepped our sessions up a notch. "Ouch!" I recoil, pulling myself out of her grip and cradling my arm against my body.

People in the hallway stop to watch. I turn back to Chantal, embarrassed. In her defense, she barely touched me. But her face is scrunched together in confusion, as she looks from my arm to my face.

"What's wrong with you?" She's borderline apologetic.

Brennan pushes past Chantal, and stands between us, shielding me. "Leave her alone, Chantal."

"I barely touched her."

"Come on, Dacie. Let's go." Brennan gently guides me away from a shocked Chantal, toward Drama.

For a moment, I feel sorry for Chantal. How was she to know I was covered in bruises under my sweater? But I keep my head up and stare straight ahead, as people in the hallways part for us. I didn't ask for Chantal to stick her nose where it didn't belong—I wanted to be alone.

We pass by Art and Music, on our way to the far corner of the basement where Drama resides. Brennan and I take a seat in the back row of class, before he speaks to me again. "Are you okay?" he whispers.

"Thank you for saving me back there."

A smile crosses his face. "You seem off lately. I just want to look out for you."

"Have you seen Tryan?" I ask. I cringe at the tone of desperation in my voice.

A frown crosses Brennan's face. "No. Did you guys get into a fight or something?"

I shake my head and turn back to the front of the room. "We're not dating, you know. It's not like that."

Brennan doesn't answer.

After a brief lecture from the teacher, she chooses volunteers to do some improv. I lean back to watch the show when the soft tune of Beethoven plays in my ears. *Tryan?* I slip out of class and follow the notes down the hall. Pausing outside the double doors of the Music room, listening to "Moonlight Sonata," I know that it has to be Tryan playing it on the other side. I can't help myself as a smile spreads across my face. Before entering the room, I take a deep breath.

"You're back!" I say, walking inside. I have so many questions for him. Why did the Senate call him back? What was he supposed to report on? Tryan stops playing and leans out from behind the piano. He looks nervous, barely smiling.

"I thought something happened to you," I say, running over. "I even went over to your house and saw—" Before I let myself go into my next line of questions I freeze. A girl stands up next to Tryan, and puts her arm on his shoulder—she's scowling at me as if I've just interrupted the maestro himself.

"Dacie," Tryan says, running his hand through his hair. "This is Liana." He looks like a child caught raiding the cookie jar.

The girl tilts closer against him; she's tall and lean like something that has just walked out of a fashion magazine. Suddenly, I realize how frumpy I look in my T-shirt, jeans, and Converse shoes. My hair feels stringy, and my nose too big. I can't stop staring at the girl standing next to Tryan, and I can't seem to make any words come out of my mouth.

"Dacie?" Tryan says again. I manage to tear my eyes away from the girl and look over at him.

"Sorry," I grumble. "Wrong room."

I back out of the Music room and practically run toward Drama. As I turn to at the end of the hall, I bump into Brennan.

"Hey. I looked over, and you were gone." He quickly replaces his smile with a thin line of concern. "What's wrong?"

"Nothing." I look back to the Music room as Tryan comes out the door, pausing when he sees Brennan and me standing together at the end of the hall. Liana is right beside him.

Brennan follows my gaze then looks back at me. "Oh, crap."

"Dacie." Tryan pleads, walking toward us.

"Listen, man," Brennan steps in front of me. "I don't think she wants to see you."

"Get out of here," Tryan says.

"What's going on out here?" Our teacher appears at the door. She looks from Brennan and me to Tryan and Liana before continuing. "Brennan and Dacie, get back to class. Tryan, don't you have a class to get to?"

Tryan's eyes flicker at me, then back to the teacher. "Yes, ma'am."

I slip into the Drama room behind Brennan, looking back. The teacher closes the door and rolls her eyes. "Boys like that are trouble, Dacie. I advise you to get back to your schoolwork."

The class snickers and my face gets hot, but I slink to the back of the class before I have to make eye contact with anyone. Brennan follows and sits next to me.

"Are you okay?" he whispers.

I cross my arms and give him a nasty look. I didn't ask for his help. I certainly don't need anyone in my personal business. Instead of answering, I open my notebook and start sketching.

"Fine." Brennan lifts his hands in the air. "Kill me for caring."

I stare down at my notebook in frustration. *Who is that girl and why is she with Tryan?* The more I think about it, the angrier I get. *Is she his girlfriend? Is she a summoner?* Thoughts swim wildly in my head like a pen full of sharks, each attacking the other for my attention. I grip the pencil in my hand tighter until it snaps, snapping me from my stupor. I look down at the paper and see a face, covered in shadows. I don't remember drawing it, and even freakier, it's moving right before my eyes.

The bell rings, and I jump from my seat. Brennan gives me a quizzical look, but I ignore him and look down at the paper. The face has stopped moving from behind the scribbles. I am seriously losing my mind.

I leave class and go straight for my car. But of course, like in most of my escape attempts, Miss Nelson hovers like a guard, near the exit.

"Dacie." She waves me over.

"What?" I respond. A frown crosses her face—or is it surprise? I have no patience for pleasantries. Why can't people just leave me alone today?

"I hear there was an incident with you and Chantal this morning."

Seriously? I shake my head. "You heard wrong."

I walk past her and push open the door. She doesn't call after me, as I cross the schoolyard into the parking lot. I know she can't make me stay; it's not as if I'm some little kid. I get to my car and fumble with my keys in my bag, dropping them on the ground. *Bah!* I grab them, and stand up, only to see Tryan holding his truck passenger door open for Liana.

"Dacie," Brennan calls out.

I'm unable to tear my eyes off Tryan, who looks in my direction while Brennan shouts after me. I wish I could disappear. Where's a demon when I need one? Brennan steps in front of me, blocking my view. *Argh!* Can't everyone just leave me alone?

"Hey, do you want to go out later tonight? We could go over some yearbook stuff and get a bite to eat?"

"Brennan, you need to—" Tryan's eyes catch mine, over Brennan's shoulder. My heart skips a beat as my voice catches in my throat. For a second, it looks like he's going to run over to me, and maybe, just maybe everything will be all right. But in the next second, Liana leans through the truck window, and kisses him on the cheek. Instead of landing its next beat, my heart trips and falls against my ribs. *Ugh.*

"What about tomorrow?" Brennan asks. "Totally friends. It'll be my treat, I promise."

"Fine," I whisper, tearing my eyes away from Tryan. I can barely form words right now. My mind is elsewhere, and I lack the energy to fight anymore. "Tomorrow."

"Awesome." Brennan beams. He waits until I get in my car and close the door, before walking away.

Tryan's truck drives away, leaving me in the parking lot, sitting still, fixated on my steering wheel. I twist my grip back and forth, repeatedly. *Get your shit together, Dacie.* I swallow my pride and look up, only to see Miss Nelson watching me from the school doors. As I drive out of the school parking lot, I manage to hold back the onslaught of tears that threatens to fall.

CHAPTER NINETEEN

"Home so early?" Katya calls from the kitchen.

I ignore Katya, and turn for the stairs. I managed to make it all the way home without crying, realizing I was ridiculous to get upset about Liana. It's not as if I'm interested in Tryan; I just need his help. My reflection in the rearview mirror of my car showed me that I look like hell, and I don't want to have to explain why because I barely understand myself.

"Come help me with the party planning," she calls again.

"No thanks."

"It's your party, not mine," she adds.

I pause on the steps, then give in, and make my way to the kitchen. Katya has the table covered in papers. Some show decorations, while others look like events. She stares at me for a moment, but looks away without mentioning my puffy eyes. *There is a god.*

"Seriously?" I say holding up a brochure for a clown company.

"I grabbed a little bit of everything when I was in the city." She shrugs. "What do I know about teenagers?"

"You never wanted kids?" I ask. It feels like a forbidden question as the words leave the end of my tongue and suddenly, the air around us feel tainted.

"Once," Katya says, grabbing at a pendant around her neck. "But that was not meant to be."

My face gets warm, and I feel foolish. "Just keep it simple," I say, pulling out a brochure from under the pile. "Like this one, just some patio lights, treats, and music."

Katya takes the brochure from me and raises an eyebrow. "That's it?"

"It's more than I ever had." I smile. "My birthdays were usually spent going through a drive-thru and eating in the car. This will definitely be extravagant."

Katya shrugs and starts cleaning off the table. "It's special, you know."

"Birthdays?"

"Yours," she says. "It lands on the equinox. Winter follows, bringing with it shorter days of light. It marks the last bit of balance we have until the next year."

"Don't sound so dreary," I say, but a shiver runs down my spine.

I turn and start back toward the stairs. Katya calls out to me one last time.

"Daciana," she says, "I know something is going on with you and that tovaros. Finding the right one is difficult—it shouldn't be such work to make things right. Perhaps we could spend the summer in Romania; you could meet others like you?"

Others?—I'm not alone? "That would be great."

I leave Katya smiling as I run up to my room.

Once alone, I lie on my bed, but instantly visions of Tryan and that girl flood my thoughts. *Gah—why can't I stop thinking about them?* I need to keep busy. I go to my desk and pull out a pad of paper, bringing up Brennan's email with the yearbook pages. I start sketching some funny cartoons to go with the photos.

As it gets darker outside, my eyelids lower, and I realize how exhausted I feel. My last sketch got a little out of control, and ended up looking like Liana. I stare at the sketch in frustration. Suddenly, her eyes blink and her hair begins to move, and before I know it, the image slightly lifts from the page.

I jump back, knocking my chair on the floor then look back at the paper—nothing. The pencil drawing is still, no longer resembling Liana at all. I rub my eyes, then I close up my sketchpad and crawl into bed.

Am I going crazy? Maybe that's what happens with this ability—you start seeing things everywhere you go. I know there's no way a demon could have been in that sketch; I just drew it. This ability feels more and more like a curse.

I think about my mom, as I lie awake. *Is this why she drank every day?* Mom wasn't what you'd call "settled." Her dancing job allowed us to move to pretty much any washed-up hole of a town. After her shifts, she'd usually party the rest of the night, and I'd get to have breakfast with a myriad of half-drunk, half-dressed men.

Rolling over in bed, I clutch my pillow. I miss her, I really do. There were moments, like when she'd wake me up at dawn and take me somewhere special, like the beach, or a café, or some other secret hideaway she had found. Those few hours we'd spend together laughing were rare, but I held on to them for the gems they were in my childhood.

I wonder how often she saw the shadows, crossing our paths, hiding in corners, or the pictures hanging on the walls. *Was that why we moved—to escape and give her a moment of peace?* What could have been so wrong about becoming a summoner that made her run in the first place?

A tap comes from my window. At first, I don't notice it, but then it comes again, and a third follows even more quickly. I jump out of bed and peer into the darkness. Down below, illuminated by the lights of our front steps, Tryan waves to me. But I don't wave back. I raise a finger at him to wait, even though I'd rather give him a different one.

I hesitate at the front door, then take a deep breath and walk outside.

"What?" I ask, crossing my arms, staying on the porch, out of reach.

"I want to explain."

"I don't need an explanation," I say. "I *was* worried when I saw your place. I'm not anymore."

"You went to my place?" He scratches the back of his head, awkwardly standing in front of me. It's the first time he's acted like a teenage boy since I met him.

"I didn't want to leave, but they didn't leave me a choice."

"Who didn't?" I ask. "Liana? I can tell you're just helpless around her."

"Liana? No, why would she? It was the Senate. They sent some people to retrieve me."

"What Senate?"

"The Tovaros High Senate."

"What does that have to do with that girl?"

Tryan lets out a loud sigh. "Liana is my babysitter now. It's my consequence for helping an underage summoner cross demons over from the netherworld."

"You're being punished for the demons I let through?"

He nods.

"But you didn't help me. I let that imp and ogre through on my own."

"The Senate doesn't see it that way."

I tap my foot on the porch, as Tryan watches me. I feel sorry that he's in trouble for something I did, but that doesn't explain how familiar he and this Liana seem to be. Maybe she's the girl he spent last year with—another summoner.

"You've obviously met your *babysitter* before. She's rather friendly for someone who's supposed to be watching you."

A flicker of hurt crosses his face. "It's not like that."

"I don't care." I know I sound like a silly girl, pouting as I tap my foot, so I straighten myself up to regain my composure. "Is she staying at your house?"

"Yes," Tryan says, looking at the ground.

My chest tightens and I can feel my stomach burning. Visions of Liana, the long-legged model, stream through my head. Liana sitting on Tryan's couch. Liana in Tryan's bedroom.

"I guess I'll see you two around." I turn and open the door.

"Wait!" Tryan calls out. I pause with my hand on the handle. "Can I see you tomorrow night?"

"I'm busy," I say, opening the door. "I have a date." Tryan doesn't answer. I walk inside and close the door, without looking back at Tryan; I can't. Instead, I brace my back against the door. *Why am I acting so stupid?*

I return to my bedroom, close my curtains, and go to bed. All night I toss and turn. A few times when I wake up, it feels like someone's outside, watching the house. But when I get up to look out my window, all I see are shadows playing together in the streets.

CHAPTER TWENTY

The next day is terrible. Actually, it just plain sucks. I wake up late, hurry out of the house, my hair half-brushed, and I'm still in the same clothes from the night before. I'm late for the first period, which means I have to walk in front of the entire class looking like death warmed over. Worse—Brennan's beaming at me from his desk, which reminds me of our date tonight. *Fantastic.* Thankfully, Tryan's not in class.

At lunch, I search for a place to sit where no one will see me. That's when I see them: Tryan and Liana. She's laughing aloud in some twinkling, crystalline voice while she sits close—a little too close—to Tryan.

Someone bumps into me, and I stumble a few steps forward. Tryan's eyes look up and catch mine, but I quickly look away and disappear into the crowd. I find a quiet spot near the wall, sit down, and stare at my food. I've lost the little bit of appetite I have left, even though my stomach rumbles in protest. I grab my fruit bowl and pick at a grape with my fork.

Brennan slides in across from me. *How did he find me?* I glance at him quickly, and then turn my attention back to my grape.

"I thought that tonight we could go down to Marcotte's?" he says.

Marcotte's is a local restaurant, known for its dim lights and romantic music. Katya and Constantine took me there one night, shortly after moving here. The entire meal scene is just not my style. Plus, it's more of a *let's go steady* kind of restaurant than it is a *we're just friends* place.

"That's a little fancy for a hangout," I grumble. "I thought this was just friends?"

"It is," he says quickly. "The arcade will be too busy to get any work done."

"How about a good old coffee shop," I say, "like the Common."

"Isn't that for old people?" Brennan scrunches up his nose.

I have to laugh aloud at this. "We're not six, Brennan. I'm sure people our age go there. It'll be quieter than the arcade, and more in the friend-zone."

"Fine," Brennan says. "I'll pick you up at—"

"Uh, uh, uh," I tsk. "Friend-zone, remember?"

"Friends pick up friends," Brennan argues.

Tryan and Liana walk down the aisle of the cafeteria. He's looking all around before his eyes fall on me, and hold mine, making my heart slam against my ribs, faster and faster. Then Liana stands in between us and I tear my eyes away.

I quickly look at Brennan and speak louder than usual. "Yeah, sure, pick me up at seven."

"Awesome!" Brennan beams.

I look back at Tryan, but Liana's pulling him out of the cafeteria. *Grrr.* I feel the instinct to jump from my chair and attack, but Chantal and Sophie sit down, blocking them from my view. Chantal stares from Brennan to me, and then back again, while Sophie looks up and smiles at the both of us.

"What's up tonight?" she asks.

"I've got football first," Brennan says. "Then I'm busy."

"You should come with us," Sophie says, leaning toward me.

"I'm not really into football."

"Everyone in high school loves football," Brennan presses. "What don't you like?"

I shrug. "I've never gone."

"What! Then you have to come. Sophie, you're bringing this girl to practice."

Chantal's face drops, but I bet mine looks worse. Football. Seriously. I go back to playing with my grape while Brennan drones on about all the things he wants to do this year with the yearbook. My mini-revenge didn't make me feel any better, leaving me with a lump in my throat. I pick up my untouched tray of food and stand.

"Going already?" Brennan asks.

"I should go get some homework done if we're going out tonight," I lie.

"Good thinking," he says, "see you later."

On my way out Miss Nelson is waiting for me.

"You can't avoid me forever," she says. "I'd appreciate a talk in my office."

I sigh. I deserve this for how I acted yesterday but still slink through her office door and drop myself into a chair. Her desk has a stack of manila folders on it, but the one that draws my attention is pulled to the side, and has the name CANTAR printed at the top.

"I don't like how we communicated yesterday," she begins. "I like to think when one gives respect, they deserve it back."

I shift in my seat and force myself to meet her eyes. The brown surrounding her pupil is dark and intense as it stares back at me, unrelenting.

"I understand this is a hard year for you, but I hate to see you fall apart. You have such potential, Dacie. Sometimes jumping into relationships within the same year as a personal tragedy is not a good idea."

"Tryan and I are not together." The words sound foreign as they come out of my mouth, though I can't seem to stop them from spilling out. They leave behind a gaping hole, which aches in my chest.

Miss Nelson raises an eyebrow, causing her flawless skin to crease along her forehead. "Really? I'm surprised."

"It wasn't meant to be," I grumble, fighting back my emotions as they threaten to erupt.

"So there wasn't any real connection then?"

I pause, remembering the first time we touched, how an electrical current ran through our fingers. But that was more pain than a connection. Then there was the kiss in the woods, and Tryan's utter shock and discomfort by it. That should have been a red flag as well. But that dance at school. He didn't have to, but he wanted it. I'm sure I saw it in his eyes. I shake my head. Who am I kidding? You can find anything you want if you look hard enough for it. I learned that chasing after my mother for the majority of my life. But convincing yourself it exists doesn't make it real.

"No. There wasn't a real connection."

She purses her lips together, as she leans toward me. "I won't lie. I'm glad you aren't involved. Boys like Tryan aren't always the right match. He has a file here of his own, and has had quite the past as well. It's best you each work separately on yourselves before getting involved."

The weight of her words pushes me down even lower than I felt before. It was foolish to have feelings for someone I barely know, but how am I supposed to control whom I like?

"I can see you're still in the dumps about this," Miss Nelson continues. "I don't want you becoming withdrawn. Do you have other friends you can socialize with?"

"I was invited to go watch football after school." The prospect is still unappealing.

"That's great," she says, slapping her hands together. "Just try to keep yourself busy, and don't ignore me. My door is always open."

Just as I stand, a high-pitched giggle assaults my ears; I instantly know who it is: Liana. She and Tryan walk past the office door, arm-in-arm, and I can feel my entire body tense up.

"I'm sorry," Miss Nelson says, her hand resting on my shoulder. Its warmth is settling. "I didn't know there was something else going on. You know what? Why don't you take the rest of the afternoon off?"

"Really?"

"I'll send an email to your teachers right now. Go, clear your mind, but don't miss out on some healthy socializing today. Deal?"

I nod. I have no idea where I'm going, but anywhere away from Tryan and Liana works for me.

CHAPTER TWENTY-ONE

The best way to clear my head is to go for a drive, and I've just gotten total clearance to do it. In times like these, I wish my mom were here. I don't even have a grave I can visit her at here on the East Coast, so I have to make do. I take myself to the cemetery.

The town cemetery is situated on the outskirts of town. I'm not sure why we push our dead aside, away from our day-to-day thoughts. It doesn't make them disappear, but I guess it makes it easier than driving past them each day.

I park outside the rusted iron gates and stare up through the entrance. Older cemeteries didn't account for roads, though they were carved out afterward. I can see the teetering gravestones perched at the edge of the road, and have no interest in driving on top of what rests beneath.

As I get out of the car, a dark flash zips past, brushing against my cheek like a cold breeze. I jump back, and turn just as it disappears through the gates, up the path, and between the gravestones. I should have known a cemetery would be a shadow playground.

My sneakers crunch against the crisp autumn leaves that cover the ground, leaving the trees reaching up to the sky with their barren limbs. I walk past gravestones covered in moss, as the land sluggishly reclaims itself, their clutching tendrils tracing the letters of those who lie below. Some are so plain that they're nothing more than a rectangle standing erect, while others are elaborate with tiny lambs or tall angels carved from the stone watching me as I pass by.

When I see it, towering above all others and set deep in the cemetery, I immediately know this is why I've come. It's an impressive monument, looming far above me, mounted on a pedestal of marble. Her face is stoic as she stares straight ahead and her arms reach out in front of her, as if she's looking for something. Could it be her freedom from a family legacy that haunted her, or would it simply be her escape into the next life?

Mom's grave back in California was simple; I was going to choose a headstone that sat flat against the ground, that way whomever she was running from would never find her. But Katya convinced me to get something that stood up. The irony of it all strikes me now; only in death is she free to stand up tall and proud and stay in one place. At least she gets to stay where it's warm.

Before my emotions can sink in, another dark flash zips past me, but this one disappears behind the angel. I chase after it, but instead of seeing the flash, I notice a mausoleum a few rows over. There are other mausoleums in the cemetery, but this one has my family name on it: CANTAR.

As I approach the mausoleum, I notice more words under the name: *Ours is not for judgment, but for balance.* It's just like the *Book of Summoning.* Above the mausoleum sits an angel holding a sword on its lap and a set of scales between its hands.

"Interesting family," someone pipes up from behind me.

I jump and turn to face an old man in coveralls. He has a logo of the town crest on his shirt; he must work here at the cemetery.

"Who?"

"That name there," he says. "Cantar; it means balance. They're one of the founding families of the town."

I nod and look back at the mausoleum: 'balance.' Katya's words ring in my ears, *"A summoner's job is to balance good and evil."*

"Lots of interesting stories in this place," he says. "If only the dead could talk."

"So they say," I say, turning back to him, but he's already sauntering away.

I look back at the mausoleum and smile. I've found a place that links back to Mom that I can visit anytime I want. But I can't spend all my time in a cemetery, as I have a paper to write for history class. First, I have to watch my first football practice.

I hesitate at the gate to Greystone Field, where in fall the football team trains and in summer track and field takes place. The football field sits in the center of the track below the stands that flank it near the entrance. On the other side, hidden by trees and a chain link fence, is the road that leads to the expressway and out of town. The stands are scattered with people, dressed in team colors with streamers, hats, and face paint. They're like a small tribe of crazy fans, a culture all their own. I've never seen so much pomp in my life and can only compare it to the businessmen at Mom's dance clubs, where I used to peek through the curtain, while hanging backstage when I was too young to stay home alone.

When I enter the field, Sophie waves me over to the bleachers with her usual chipper demeanor. Brennan is standing in front of her and Chantal, leaning on one leg while he holds his helmet. He has black smudges across his cheeks that move with that addicting grin of his. I smile and wave back. Luckily, my afternoon in the cemetery put me in a good mood. I make my way over, awkwardly balancing as I walk along the bleacher, and then plop down next to Sophie.

"You made it." Brennan grins. "Maybe I'll get a touchdown for you."

My stomach turns. "I thought this was just practice."

"Ignore him." Sophie rolls her eyes. "He and Zack are always showing off."

Brennan puts on his helmet, and I jump as he hits the side with his fists and makes a grunting sound. He turns and runs toward the field filled with other gray jerseys and tight blue pants.

"I don't get football," I say, watching the boys tackle each other down on the field.

"What's not to get?" Sophie smiles. "Boys in tight pants and bevies." She holds up a smoothie cup, but I'm betting that's not what's inside. "Want some?" She holds the cup out to me.

I shake my head. Even though they are no paintings here, I have no urge to experience a replay of the arcade.

"More for me." Chantal reaches over and grabs the cup.

I notice someone is watching us over where the school meets the chain link fence that surrounds the field. The curly dark hair makes me think it's Miss Nelson, but the person moves before I can be sure.

"I'll be right back."

I run up the hill to the spot on the fence looking for where Miss Nelson went. Was she checking up on me? I spot her not too far away, standing by her car at the edge of a group of trees. I'm about to call out when I realize she's talking to someone.

"It's not a good time," she says.

No one answers.

"Yes, they've been separated. I understand your pleasure in that. But I still think this is a bad idea. It's not my fault when you took her mother it sucked up all your strength. You should have known better than to mess with a paranoid summoner."

Summoner? My entire body goes rigid, and I lose all sensation except for the heartbeat in my chest, now thundering in my ears. How can she know those things? I grip the fence tighter, trying to see with whom she is talking.

"If the boy is not the tovaros we can slow down. Let me get a little more information about her aunt, then you will have everything you need. She trusts me now."

The metal of the fence bites into my skin as anger surges through my limbs making my body shake. The fence quivers against its posts. She's talking about me. And she's right, I trusted her. Her. Tryan. Hell, I even trusted my mother once. When will I learn?

Miss Nelson spins around as the fence vibrates louder. Her eyes widen when she sees me. But it's not guilt that sits behind those dark brown eyes—it's fear. Behind her, shadows move upward through the trees and a flock of blackbirds bursts into the sky.

"What are you doing?" I yell at her.

She looks from the trees back to me, then pulls open her car door and jumps inside. Her tires squeal, as her tiny sports car speeds away from the parking lot.

"What's wrong?" Sophie's voice comes from behind me.

I turn to her and shake my head, unsure where I would even begin to explain.

She puts a hand on my shoulder. "Is that Miss Nelson speeding away?" Chantal asks, grabbing the fence next to me. "You look like you might kill her."

"She doesn't know when to mind her own business," I grumble.

"I totally get it," Chantal says. "Damn adults. Think they know everything."

Even though I'm pissed off, I can't help but smile. For the first time Chantal and I agree on something—though she has no idea why. Miss Nelson does know something. And I'm going to find out what.

CHAPTER TWENTY-TWO

After practice, Brennan showers and then opts to ride with me. He talks the entire time, but I barely listen. The Miss Nelson situation is still confusing, but I have to play the part with Brennan while I come up with a plan. When we get to the Common, he pops out a laptop and gets right to business with some of his yearbook ideas.

"I'm impressed," I say at the end of his speech. "You really are organized."

"Did you think the whole yearbook thing was just a ruse to hang out?"

I burst into laughter again, which makes Brennan smile even more.

"I'll grab us some coffees," he says, getting up. "I brought a little something we can slip into them, too." He flashes me a silver flask from his pocket.

"Just a black coffee is good for me." Does no one around her know how to socialize without alcohol?

I watch as Brennan walks away, his athletic build shifting with every step under his sweater, which hangs over the top of his white T-shirt. His jeans hang just slightly off his hips, revealing the top band of his underwear when he raises his arm at the barista. When I look back up at his face, he's looking at me.

My face blushes and I look away quickly, toward the windows of the café. I instantly wish I had kept staring at Brennan. Tryan's old truck pulls up across the street. My heart skips against my chest, and I can feel my hands start to sweat. Tryan helps Liana out of the truck, and they walk into the movie theater across from us.

Brennan slides back into his seat, blocking my view. He sets a steamy cup in front of me, and I stare down at the hot liquid, watching the vapors as they rise from the surface. "What's wrong?" he asks. "Is it the alcohol? We don't have to—"

"No," I say, "it's not that." My eyes flicker past him, out to Tryan's truck. Brennan spins around in his chair, following my gaze.

"I see the problem." Brennan turns back to me. "That guy's a jerk. You can do better, Dacie."

"It's a long story," I explain. "He was supposed to help me with something—I thought he was my friend." I look back down at my coffee. Maybe Tryan is a jerk. Just because he claims to be stuck with Liana, doesn't mean he had to avoid me.

"Pass me that flask," I whisper to Brennan. He flashes me a smile, and I can feel something bump my leg. I reach down as the cold steel brushes against my fingers.

I slip some of the alcohol into my coffee and watch Brennan do the same thing. A small smile plays at the edge of his lips, and I realize how cute he is now that he doesn't have all his friends around asking so many questions.

After an hour of looking at different yearbook layouts, the flask is empty, and I'm left feeling relaxed and happy. I haven't felt this good for a long time. Brennan is looking happy too, but I think it's because he has someone to show his photos.

"You really surprised me," I say. "I thought you were just all jock."

"It's photography I like best," he says. "But this year I thought it would be cool to get into the graphic design part as well— you know, start to prep for college."

"College seems so far away."

"It's our last year," Brennan laughs. "It's closer than you think."

"I don't ever think about college," I say. "I don't ever think much about the future."

"Oh, yeah," Brennan says, looking down at the table and fumbling with his hands. "I guess you wouldn't."

I shift uncomfortably in my seat, waiting for the inevitable barrage of questions about my mom, but Brennan reaches out for my hand instead. His touch feels warm, which intermingled with the alcohol, sends heated sensations throughout my fingers.

"Why don't you ever ask me about her?" I ask.

Brennan looks back at me. "Because that's your past," he says. "If you want to share it with me, you will."

His stare is so invasive that I look away, intimidated by the hunger that's firing in his eyes. I turn my head toward a canvas hanging on the wall above us, which is ironically a painting of a cute café on a street.

Brennan's grip tightens on my hand, and I glance back at him. "I need to tell you," he says, his cheeks a little redder than usual. "I like you. I think we could have something special here."

I look away back at the painting and form my words carefully. *Was it just my imagination, or did the shadows of the café stretch out farther onto the street?*

"Brennan," I say, "I think you're cool, and tonight I've had a lot of fun. But I think we should stay friends and hang out a little more before we jump into anything."

"You barely knew Tryan," he says, gripping tighter on my fingers. I pull my hand back and hide it in my lap. I can't look back at Brennan, because I know he's right. "You let that guy treat you like crap," he continues, "and you still want to wait for him."

"I'm not waiting for anyone." I tear my hand away from him and look back to the painting, angry at Brennan's words and angrier with myself. I am not going to let myself turn into my mother. I am not weak. I practically raised myself. If Brennan thinks I'm after Tryan, either I'm giving off that vibe or he's just jealous. Either way, I'm uncomfortable.

The shadows in the painting get larger, then begin to shift and swirl through the other colors, until the entire painting is covered in a black streak. I shift back in my seat, away from the wall.

"Why won't you look at me when I'm talking to you?" he asks, and I quickly glance at him as he turns toward the painting. "What's so interesting up there?"

"Don't," I say to Brennan, my head fuzzy from the alcohol.

He leans toward the painting and looks at it closely. I watch as something dark reaches out, grabbing onto the bottom of the frame. At the same time, Brennan reaches up and pokes at the canvas.

"What the—?" His face drops as the canvas pulls out with his finger.

"Brennan," I warn, "don't play around with that, we'll get into trouble."

He turns back with a confused look, still trying to pull his finger away from the canvas. Near his face, long sharp claws extend from the hands that reach out from the painting. A matted head of hair with two long horns, like barren tree branches, thrust out from behind its head. Two beady red eyes look down at me, followed by the flash of jagged white teeth.

"What's happening with this painting?" Brennan stands up and leans closer. "Someone must have put glue—"

"No!" I yell at Brennan, but it's too late.

The creature lurches from the painting, knocking Brennan over. I scream as it jumps from the table onto the floor. It looks back at me with a growl, then disappears out the door nearly knocking over two customers.

I drop to the floor, next to Brennan and lift his head into my lap. A trickle of blood runs down his cheek from where the creature attacked him. A barista runs over to us, looking at the ripped painting, then down at Brennan. "What happened here?" she asks, pointing at the painting.

"You didn't see anything?"

"Yeah, I saw you and your buddy disturbing everyone in here," she says, picking up the flask, which landed on the floor next to Brennan. She takes a whiff and flinches. "Real nice. You kids can't be old enough to drink? I'm calling the cops. And somebody is going to pay for that painting."

The cops arrive with an ambulance, and shortly after Brennan's parents show up. Half an hour later, Brennan gets the green light to go home, and under the scrutiny of his mother, he comes and says goodbye to me.

"Sorry about all this," he says, awkwardly rubbing a hand against the bandage on his cheek. Not deep enough for stitches. Phew. "Crappy first date."

"Just friends, remember?"

"Right," Brennan says, and a flash of disappointment crossing his face. "What happened in there anyway? One minute I'm talking to you, the next I look at that painting—and I swear something hit me on the head."

"Oh, yeah," I say. "Uh, you poked that painting and it fell off the wall."

"Damn," he says. "No wonder my mom is so pissed. She said I

have to pay her back for it. I guess I'll see you at school."

Brennan leaves and I'm relieved that no one's been able to reach Katya. Seeing as Brennan took responsibility for the painting, I should be able to leave. But before I can disappear, the doors of the movie theater open up and Tryan and Liana exit with the other attendees. The ambulance and police car quickly draw their attention. Tryan spots me and runs over with Liana close on his heels.

"What happened?" he asks, reaching out to me. I step back.

"Just a public disturbance warning."

"Have you been drinking?" Tryan asks. I look away just as Brennan's dad passes us with the broken painting. I guess if he has to buy it, he's entitled to the salvage.

"What's going on?" Liana says, pushing Tryan out of the way. "What did you do here?"

"It's none of your business," I say, staring down Liana.

"We need to know, little girl," Liana says, staring down at me.

"Who are you calling—"

"Whoa, you two. Stop it," Tryan says, getting between the two of us. "Dacie, please, tell me what got out."

I throw the dirtiest look I can muster at Liana, and turn to Tryan. "I don't know. Something with long claws, tiny beady eyes, and long horns that looked like tree branches."

"A wendigo?" Liana asks, honestly looking shocked. It makes me smile. "How could you be so stupid?" she continues.

My smile turns into a frown.

"This is why I didn't want to leave Dacie alone," Tryan says, crossing his arms and blocking Liana. "I told you, she needs me."

"I don't *need* anyone," I snap.

"She's out of control," Liana mutters. "What she needs is a swift kick in the—"

"What did you say about me?" I say, trying to push Tryan out of the way.

"Liana!" Tryan says. "Take the truck—I'll meet you there. You need to get things ready; we're hunting tonight."

Liana narrows her eyes at me and lets out a huff, before turning on her heels and getting into the truck. She spins the tires until they squeal before taking off. Tryan turns to me, and I have a stupid grin on my face from what I feel is my first victory against Liana.

"What's your problem?" He looks down at me with his lips pursed, and his eyebrows pushed together. "I can't believe you were this careless."

I step back for a moment. I didn't expect our reunion to be like this. "What's so terrible about a wendigo?" I ask. "It looked freaky, but let's find it and paint it back."

"Dacie." Tryan sighs. "Wendigoes are nothing like imps. They're dangerous to hunt, and they're really smart."

"What's so dangerous about them?" I ask, remembering the beady red eyes, the long claws, and sharp teeth.

"They eat people," he says.

CHAPTER TWENTY-THREE

The drive home with Tryan suffocates me. My fuzzy head is slowly getting clearer, and the sharper it gets, the more embarrassed I become. Especially since Tryan is not talking—at all. He's the total opposite of Brennan. Finally, we pull up to my dark house.

"Is your aunt already asleep?"

I shrug and leave him in the car, too humiliated to speak. I stumble as I reach the steps to the porch, but Tryan is there to catch me. I turn to him, smelling his woodsy aroma. I have the weirdest need to know what brand it is, but all I can do is stare at his face. His lips are still firmly set in a straight line, but his eyes look softly down at me.

A sudden feeling of sadness washes over me, and I start to push him away. A sob escapes my lips. I cover my face to make sure the tears stay back. No tears. No crying. Get a grip.

"What's wrong?" he asks, pulling me back against him.

I swallow back my emotions, pushing them down as far as I can. "You hate me."

His hand runs down my long hair as a chuckle escapes his lips. "I don't hate you," he whispers.

"You like Liana more." I take a deep breath.

"Dacie," he says, "you're drunk. Let's get you inside and to bed."

"Yes," I slur. "You need to run off to your girlfriend." The sarcasm drools from my words; I want him to hurt so he knows how I feel.

"She's not my girlfriend," he says with an edge to his voice. He opens the front door and pulls me inside. "Katya!" he calls out, walking ahead and leaving me in the front entry.

I close the door behind us, then see something move next to me and jump back. It's only my reflection in the mirror. I start to laugh, but the sound catches in my throat. My reflection looks eerily like my mother. A shudder runs through my body; I look like my mother after a night of drinking. My hair is disheveled and my eyes are vacant as I escape my reality.

My stomach lurches and I run for the guest bathroom next to Katya's studio. I stop at the sink, managing to hold everything in, and see my reflection again. *I am not her.* I wash my face and brush my hair back into a ponytail.

I have no idea where Tryan is, but I don't care. I go up to my bedroom and crawl into my pajamas. *Why did I drink tonight?* I swore to myself I would never be like Alina and here I am starting to walk in her footsteps. I grab her picture and sit on the edge of my bed, running my finger across her face.

"You okay?" Tryan appears at my bedroom door.

I nod, not looking away from my mother's photo.

"I found a note," he says, bringing a piece of paper to me and sitting next to me.

Daciana–
I drove Constantine to the airport. Be back late tomorrow
morning.
–Katya

"Where is Constantine going?" Tryan asks.

I shrug and lean back on my bed, clutching my mother's picture to my chest.

"Are you sure you're okay?" he asks, turning toward me.

"I was a fool tonight," I say. "I thought I could have a normal life. But I never will, will I? Look at my mother; she ran away to escape this life, and in the end, she ended up the same way as she would have, had she never left."

"Don't say that," Tryan says. "You have me. Your mother was alone."

"My mother had me," I say, sitting up and putting the photo back on my nightstand. "And I don't have you—you have someone else. And you should go see her."

Tryan bites his lip before looking down at his hands. He stands up and starts to pace the room, then looks out my bedroom window, into the darkness of the woods behind the house.

"It's too dark out to go looking for a wendigo," he says, running a hand through his hair.

Tryan reaches into his pocket and grabs his cell phone before going out into the hallway. I watch him, confused for a moment, as I lean as far as I can toward the door to listen.

"Yeah, it's me," he says. "Listen, I'm staying here … No, we should wait … No, I don't think that's a good idea … Listen, I said no, I'm staying here … No, you aren't coming over … I'll see you tomorrow."

I scramble back onto the other side of my bed and look away from the door. Tryan comes back into my room, looking frustrated. Why is he staying? It doesn't make any sense.

"So?" He runs his hands through his hair again. "If you want, I could stay here."

"For the night?"

"Yeah." He bites his lip again. "I mean, I'll sleep on the floor—I just thought that you could use some company, after tonight and all. But if you don't want me to, I'll go."

"So you don't hate me after all?" I ask, holding my breath as I play with the edge of my pajama shirt.

"I never could." He sits back beside me.

The air in my lungs slowly exhales as relief falls over me. I turn my face up to Tryan's, only to find his eyes fixated on me.

"You were mad at me tonight," I whisper.

"You were out with another boy."

"You were out with another girl," I say, my heart tightening for a moment as I remember him and Liana getting out of his truck and going to the movies.

"I felt like I was going to go crazy the entire time I was in the movie," he says. "I saw you two at the coffee shop."

I snort. "I don't like Brennan. Not in the same way."

"The same way as what?" A smile plays at the edge of his lips.

"The same way I would like my tovaros," I tease, bumping my shoulder into his. "If I ever find him."

"Poor Brennan," Tryan says. A flash of jealousy mixed with satisfaction washes over his face. "He'll never be your tovaros."

My stomach twists from the sound of his deep voice, his last words coming out broken and quiet. "Why not?"

Tryan leans closer to my ear. "Because I'm yours."

His breath cascades across my ear and settles at the nape of my neck, and I let out a tiny gasp as shivers run down my skin. Tryan reaches over and touches the other side of my face as he brushes his lips against my ear and down to my neck.

His soft kisses trail up my cheek, and cross over to my lips. I lean in toward Tryan, reaching my hands up around his neck, pulling him closer. His arms reciprocate and wrap around my waist. It feels like forever before our kiss ends. There's a tranquility in those moments, which gives me a needed break from all the madness my life has become.

"I've wanted to kiss you since I met you that day in the hallway," he says.

"I was so mean that day." I cover my face and lean back on my pillows.

"You were so feisty," he says, pulling my hands away as he lies beside me. "You even zapped me. It was intriguing, but, I have to say, I like you like this too."

"Intoxicated?" I say. "Don't get your hopes up."

"Not that part," Tryan says, tracing a finger down my nose to my lips. "You're so open and nice, not a combo you usually portray."

"Hey," I say, hitting him with a pillow. I squeal aloud as he tickles me.

We end up face-to-face, and I stare up into his eyes. "Can we kiss again?"

"One more," he says. "I don't want to be accused of taking advantage of a girl under the influence."

I lean in, feeling the familiar pull between us. The second kiss is just as good as the first. I can feel a warmth wash across the inside of my body, trailing down my limbs all the way to my toes. As it resonates, it feels like little fireworks are going off underneath my skin. I smile to myself. *Fireworks are better than shocks.*

CHAPTER TWENTY-FOUR

I wake up in the familiar darkness of my room, clutching my pillow against my cheek. I remember Tryan slept over last night. Butterflies jump around my stomach. I open my eyes and look for him, but both sides of the bed around me are empty.

"Daciana-a-a," a voice calls out to me.

I sit up and my heart slams against my chest. The hairs on my arm stand alert like little radars. A howl of wind comes from my bedroom window, pushing the long curtains away with it.

I relax and get out of bed to close the window, but as I pull it down, I see Tryan running across the backyard. *Where is he going in the dead of night?*

"Tryan!" I call out, but he doesn't hear me.

I run out of my bedroom and down the stairs into the kitchen.

The patio door is wide open, and Tryan's white shirt disappears into the trees.

"Daciana-a-a-a," the deep voice calls out to me again. This time it's behind me.

I freeze and force my body to slowly turn and face my visitor. Nothing is behind me except the long hallway to the front door—and Katya's studio. *Creak.* The doorway to the studio slowly opens, stopping halfway. The room is dark, but I can make out a dark figure standing next to the window.

"Who are you?" I cry out.

The figure moves and jumps out the window.

"Wait!"

I run into the studio and look out the window.

The dark figure hurries across the lawn toward the woods.

"No!"

I climb out the window, chasing after the figure into the woods.

The trees are so dense that the moonlight disappears as soon as I enter the woods. I stumble into trees and against brush. A branch whips my leg, tearing through my nightgown. I yelp as it bites into my flesh.

"Tell me your name," I yell out desperately, nearly about to give up.

"My Daciana," the voice echoes through the trees, rustling the leaves as my name carries across a gust of wind so strong I can't catch my breath. Suddenly, a flash of white light fills the air and everything is gone.

"Ahhh!" I sit up in bed and open my eyes. My heart beats out of control, and my skin pulses hot. Throwing myself back onto my pillows, I try to catch my breath. It *was* just a dream. I roll over to see if I woke up Tryan, but I'm alone in bed. I run my hand along the cold sheet where I saw him last. Did he stay the night or was he only pacifying a drunken friend?

But that kiss—oh, that kiss. I touch my lips, as if the sensation could bring back the fireworks from the night before. Nothing happens, but it doesn't take away from how real it was. He said he had wanted to kiss me since he met me. He said he was mine. The butterflies are back, but this time I know I'm not dreaming.

Flipping back over, I survey my room. Daylight streams through my bedroom window and the smell of bacon fills my nostrils. I jump out of bed and get dressed.

As I pull up my pants, I notice dried blood. I lean down and rub the mark, but my skin is tender—it's where the branch cut my leg in my dream. No, that can't be it. I pull my pants over it and put it in the back of my mind.

Downstairs, I find Tryan cooking in the kitchen. His dark hair sweeps across his eyes as he looks up at me from the sizzling bacon in the frying pan.

"Hungry?" he asks, his eyes burning as they look into mine.

I nod, watching as he works away. His shirt clings against his chest, showing the muscles underneath that flex with every movement he makes. I want to reach out and run my hands across that shirt, but I hold the impulse inside.

"I missed you this morning," I say, leaning over the counter, watching him cook.

"I'm not going anywhere." Tryan flashes me a smile. "I stayed by your side all night."

He leans forward and kisses me, and the same feeling of fireworks fills me up.

A bang at the patio door interrupts our moment. I look up and see Liana standing on the other side of the glass, with one hand on her hip and another carrying a large duffel bag.

"Did you invite her?" I ask, unable to hold back the sharp edge from my voice.

"No," Tryan says, flipping bacon. "But we can't ignore her now. I'm pretty sure she sees us."

"We could still pretend." I sigh and go to the door, opening it a crack.

"What do you want?" I ask.

"Tryan and I have work to do," Liana says, narrowing her eyebrows and holding up the duffel bag.

I roll my eyes and slide the patio door open all the way. Liana pushes past me and throws the duffel bag on the counter.

"Seeing as you were too busy to do our job last night," she says, "I did some recon. The wendigo is most likely hiding out in the woods.

Nothing came across the police scanners all night, so I'll just assume we're lucky that it didn't do any damage. That being the case, it's even more vital we find it today, because tonight it's going to be starving."

"First, Dacie and I are going to have breakfast," Tryan says. "Bacon?"

"Tryan," she says. "You aren't taking this seriously. This really is her problem, not ours; I'm just trying to—"

"What do you mean it's my problem?" I ask, crossing my arms.

"You're the one that let it out." Liana turns to me, with raised eyebrows. "Like, seriously, who taught you summoning?"

"The Senate said what Dacie does is my problem," Tryan says, passing me my plate. "She isn't seventeen yet."

"What?" Liana looks confused, her perfectly painted lips are hanging open in disbelief. I almost laugh aloud. "How is that possible?"

I shrug and bite into my bacon as Tryan sits beside me. Liana stares at us both from the other side of the counter.

"Do you not get how serious this is?" Liana throws her hands up in the air. "An underage summoner, with abilities, letting out wendigoes. Only experienced summoners can handle that level of demon. I thought you were stupid, but you're really just—"

"Don't call me 'stupid,'" I say mid-chew.

"Is this why I'm here?" Liana says, her eyes getting wider. "Because you can't handle an underage summoner. *ARGH!* I had to cancel my anniversary plans because of this! Tryan, I'm sick of bailing you and your summoners out of trouble."

She throws up her hands again and grabs a piece of bacon off Tryan's plate. I watch Liana carefully as she eats in frustration.

"Your anniversary?" I ask. "You have a boyfriend?"

"Of course I have a boyfriend, and he's a summoner like you," Liana huffs, flicking her long, blond hair over her shoulder. "But he's not letting out demons on a whim; he's *actually* trained to do his job."

I look down at my plate, suddenly feeling foolish and childish. Liana's right, I have no idea what I'm doing, and now people are at risk because of me.

"You forget; you're not the only one who will be held responsible for this."

"Maybe I should come help," I say.

"What do you know about any of this?" Liana dramatically shrugs.

"I'm learning," I shoot back.

"Okay, girls," Tryan speaks up. "Liana—back off. Dacie—you need to get to school. Liana and I have experience and wendigoes are dangerous. We'll drop you off on our way out."

"Fine," I grumble, flashing a look of disdain at Liana. She scrunches her nose at me, and I stifle the urge to punch it.

CHAPTER TWENTY-FIVE

At school, Tryan lets me out his door and gives me a kiss before he leaves. I wave as he and Liana drive off to find the wendigo.

"What was that?" I jump as Brennan's voice comes from behind me.

I spin around and see him glaring at me.

"Uh, it was just a ride to school," I say, looking down and walking past him.

"A ride?" Brennan grumbles. "Are you kidding me? That was a kiss. After what that guy did to you, you're still going to chase after him?"

"It was a misunderstanding," I say, as Brennan follows me.

"As in you misunderstood what a loser he is?"

"It's none of your business," I say, stopping at my locker. I open the door and block Brennan out of my sight.

"I can't believe you," Brennan seethes. "You're obsessed with him when he has a girlfriend. I didn't think you were that kind of girl."

I look around the hallway and see our classmates stopping and whispering as Brennan's voice gets higher. I can feel my skin crawl with the more people he attracts. Right now I just want to run and hide.

"Next you'll be whining about how there aren't any nice guys out there."

"*Brennan*," I warn. My palms are getting sweaty as the entire hallway watches us now. My body heats up with my anger, but I close my locker door and turn for Art. Every step I take, I use to calm myself down. *Breathe, Dacie.*

"The saying is right," Brennan yells after me. "Nice guys finish last."

I walk faster. I need to put as much distance between Brennan and me as I possibly can before I —

"You're no better than your mom. I heard she was a —"

That's it! I spin around on my heels. Some people in the hallway gasp. Others snicker. "Listen, Brennan." My voice comes out at a higher pitch than I expected. I hold my finger in the air, pointing it at him as I storm back to my locker. "I *never* asked you on a date, not once. I told you I wasn't interested in being more than friends— *multiple times*. But you never took a hint. I wouldn't call that *nice*— I'd call that *stupid*. You know what else backs my theory up? Chantal is right under your nose, begging for attention, but you're too foolish to see it."

Chantal appears in my vision, standing behind Brennan. Her face turns beet red, and she turns and runs in the other direction. Brennan's glare turns murderous as he flips me off, and storms away. Sophie and Zack, whom I hadn't noticed before, run after him and Chantal.

A few people start to clap while others burst out giggling. I stare at the floor and make my way to my class, all alone like when I started out here. It was bound to happen; all my hopes of being normal are officially gone.

Brennan doesn't return to any more classes and thankfully, I never see Chantal. I ignore the snickering that carries on the rest of the morning and by the time lunch comes, I know I won't be visiting the cafeteria. Instead, I slip into the library determined to get my paper done on the Cantars. How hard can 1,000 words be?

I find the section on history and it doesn't take me long to locate the local sub-section. There are only three books, and I take them all and find myself a table at the back of the room.

The first book talks about the history of the area. I skip ahead to the bibliography, but nothing there mentions Cantar. *Next.* The second book has a brief chapter, discussing the town's founders. It mentions the Cantars along with four others, none of which I recognize. It mentions something about a hurricane that hit the town, shortly after it was built, which killed off the other four founders. With their deaths, their family lines died as well. Wow. That's weird. The Cantars were the only ones left. I make a couple of notes and toss the book aside.

I go over to the computer and search the online catalog, typing in "`Cantar`." Nothing. Seriously? No one found the only surviving founding family of the town interesting enough to write about them?

Just for fun, I type in "`Summoning`." Nothing relevant, outside of a bunch of RPG games. I type in "`White light`." Ding. Tons of items pop up, ranging from the tunnel of light people see at death to different types of light bulbs. But one line in the search list grabs my attention: *The Brothers of the White Light*. What are the odds? I quickly write down the call number and hunt it down.

I end up in a back room lit by a pull string light. Archaic books line the shelves, and the smell of old paper hangs heavy in the air. I search the shelves and find the call number. The book is not a book at all, but rather a cardboard box. I pull it from the shelf, and a *poof* of dust fills the air. The box is surprisingly heavy and doesn't look like it has been opened for decades. I haul the box to a table and flip it open, scanning the contents.

Inside all that sits is an excerpt from an old magazine journal:

```
The Brothers of the White Light was a
monastery established in the late 1700s,
shortly after the founding of the town.
The chapel was destroyed in the hurricane
of 1780, and some say the Brotherhood
left altogether, while others say the
Brotherhood separated to chase after
those who practiced the dark arts.
```

Everything else on the article has been blacked out. What is this, the Pentagon? How could anything in this article be considered private material? I try to read the name of the magazine, but it too has been covered up.

And "dark arts"? What does that mean? The bell for classes rings and I toss the article back in the box. I'm too hungry to focus right now, and there doesn't seem to be much here for my research. All I have now are more questions.

I leave the library and pass Miss Nelson's office door on my way to class. The door is open wide and no one is inside. I remember the manila folder with "CANTAR" printed on the front. Hmmm. It would just take a second to pluck it off her desk and find all her dirty details on me inside. Maybe I'll find something about her as well.

I slip inside the office, and see the same pile of folders stacked tall. Mine isn't on the desk so it must be in the pile. There's no time to worry about not making a mess, and frankly, I'd like to ruffle Miss Nelson up a bit, thinking someone's gone through all her things. Although, I'm pretty sure I'd be her number one suspect. Finally, I come to my name in the pile. I slip out the folder and open it on the desk. It's empty. How is that possible? The last time I saw this file, it was full of paper. Could she have anticipated this and destroyed everything?

"Excuse me?" An unfamiliar voice startles me.

I spin around and come face-to-face with a teacher I've never seen before.

"Can I help you?" the woman asks.

"I was looking for Miss Nelson." I hastily turn from her desk.

"Oh, I'm sorry. You didn't hear? She left on an extended leave. It was a personal matter. I'm her replacement, Missus—"

I don't wait for the woman to finish as I push past her into the hallway. "I'm sorry. I'm late for class."

"Did you want to talk about something?" she calls after me.

"No." I shake my head, tripping over my feet as I stumble out of the office. "I'm fine." I practically run down the hall, putting as much distance between me and the new counselor as I can.

I manage to get through the rest of my day by avoiding as many people as I can, busy trying to think of who Miss Nelson could be. Is she part of this Senate Katya told me about? But that doesn't make any sense. Why would they have killed my mother? Could she be part of another group of summoners? Then why would they still be after me? None of it makes any sense.

After school, I realize I have to walk, as Tryan and Liana dropped me off. I begrudgingly carry my backpack with me and make my way home. On the way home, I pass by the cemetery and decide to take a break inside.

I keep to the edges of the cemetery, away from where a small funeral is gathering in the center. From a distance, I can see the sadness that consumes the handful of people standing nearby, and in their faces, I see my own loss.

I slip over to the Cantar mausoleum, and lean against its cold stone walls. What would my mother think if she could see me now? Would she be happy I was learning about my heritage, or furious I was getting involved in a past she tried to run away from? I let out a sigh and lean my head against the wall as I continue to watch the funeral.

"Someone you know?" I startle at the voice of the cemetery worker from over my shoulder.

"No," I grumble, tossing him a dirty look as I turn and walk behind the mausoleum.

"Oh?" He grins, standing in my way. "Just a morbid hobby?"

"What are you talking about?" I say, agitated. "Get out of my way."

He inches closer to me. "I'd watch out around these parts; strange things happen to good people around here."

"Who said I'm a good person?" I shoot back. "And what business is it of yours?"

"I'm the caretaker of these parts," he says. "This family appointed me to the task." He motions toward the family mausoleum. I look up at the angel, perched atop to guard the dead.

"I'd say you're the morbid one then," I say. "And this is my family."

He raises an eyebrow at me. "You're a Cantar? You should know more than anyone to watch out around these parts."

"How long have you been a caretaker for my family?"

He flashes me a grin. "We've buried many a summoner here."

He leans toward me, lowering his glasses. The stench of his breath burns in my nostrils, and I look into his eyes—dark eyes—clouded with swirling black smoke. I step back and bump against the mausoleum, and he leans closer to my face.

"You seem to enjoy your work." I side-step away from him, but he follows me.

"I don't know any demon that wouldn't enjoy burying a summoner."

Constantine's words run through my mind: Never trust anyone. "Get back," I sputter. "Don't touch me."

He shakes his head for a moment and steps back. "We're just talking." I shoot him an odd look, and he quickly changes his tone. "It'd be a real shame if something happened to a nice girl like you," he says. "Be careful."

"Maybe if my family knew you wanted them dead—"

"Whoa." He puts up his hands. "I don't want any of you dead, even though I'm sure you'd be delicious. If it weren't for this job, I'd be stuck in the netherworld, and the deal was no eating the bodies of summoners. No one's interested in letting a ghoul through—unless there's war or famine because of all the extra bodies lying around. We're the bottom feeders of the netherworld—living off dead flesh. When they offered me this job in exchange for a permanent possession, I jumped at the chance. Here I can feast whenever I need to."

"So that's the deal? You watch over the graves, and they let you take over this poor man's body?"

A smile creeps across the caretaker's face. "You like it?" He reaches his hand out to shake mine. "We found him a couple of towns over. He was a solitary fellow—but I wouldn't feel sorry for him. He was worse than some demons. Many a child was buried in the woods around him."

I shudder at the thought. Good riddance. "Do you know anything about the Cantar history?" I change the subject—couldn't hurt to get a first-hand perspective on things. "I mean, like way, way back to the founding days of this town."

"I was here back then; of course I didn't have a human body as that was before we had our deal. I think they were attracted to this place—the new world—what with all its demons, drifting around the west, untouched."

"Demons were free to roam, back then?"

"We were always tied to the netherworld, released through other means by those who lived on this land before any settlers. Once the summoners arrived, things became more structured. Rules were put into place. We no longer had free reign."

"I bet some demons didn't like that."

"We tried to sabotage the summoners, and they were driven out of town, long ago, shortly after the town was founded. Suspected of witchcraft—they were easy targets with their weapons and books on demonology. That was the year of the big hurricane. It wiped out the majority of the families in town. And when the Cantar's returned, their house was one of the only ones left standing. They rebuilt the town and attracted new people. Their history of witchcraft was buried with those lost in the hurricane."

"Well, we know they weren't witches." I laugh nervously. But witchcraft did sound awfully like the dark arts mentioned in the article I just read.

The caretaker shrugs and leans in toward me again, taking a deep breath as he does. "You smell different than most summoners I've met before. It's familiar, but I just can't put my finger on it."

A chill makes the hair on my arms stand up. I push past the caretaker, and a cold *zap* runs through my shoulder as it brushes against him. I quickly round back to the other side of the mausoleum, looking for a way to get away without disturbing the funeral, but I turn and see that the ceremony is ending.

As the people disperse, the boy and man from the chapel stand above the grave, reading the last rites as the coffin begins to lower. Behind the crowd's back, a flash of white light surrounds the pair and follows the coffin into the grave. As the coffin stops, the light disappears. *What was that?*

Chapter Twenty-Six

The boy and the man leave the now-empty cemetery, and I can't help but follow them. I need to see where they live and find out what they are. Could they be part of the Brotherhood of the White Light? If so, why did they come back? Maybe they never left in the first place.

They walk toward my side of town at a brisk pace. I break out in a run as I try to keep up; I'm only a few blocks away from home. As they get closer to my street, they slow down and park on the main road, next to the woods. I hide behind a post office box as they enter the woods.

I swallow, watching the woods apprehensively as the pair disappears between the trees. There's no time to worry about wendigoes or dark figures in the trees. *It's now or never.*

I slowly enter the woods, stepping carefully between logs and tall grasses. For a second I think I've already lost track of the pair, but then the boy's blond hair appears up ahead.

They go deeper into the woods while I keep my distance and stay behind the trees. Sometimes the man looks down at the ground as if he's tracking something. Other times he just stands there, looking far above, as if he expects something just to appear. After twenty minutes of slowly creeping along, I get bored and decide it's time to turn back.

Just then, the boy calls out, and I spin around in surprise. *Did they see me?* A flash of white light shines through the trees, nearly blinding me. The man is shouting at the boy, and before I can make out what they say, they disappear into the trees up ahead.

What happened? What was that light? I have to know. I take off running after them, ignoring the branches as they whip against my legs. I can still hear the man yelling something at the boy, but he's getting farther and farther away.

I stop for a breath and lean against a tree. This was one of my more wild ideas. What was I thinking, chasing two strangers into the woods? As I calm down, I realize I'm completely lost. I never considered I might need a way out of the woods.

A flash of white light zips past my face, and I duck reflexively behind the tree. Footsteps are approaching quickly, but there's no time to run. I'll have to face them or hide. I choose the latter. As I crouch between the grasses, they get within arm's length.

"I swear, Father," the boy says. "I saw it, I really did."

"I'm sure you did, Eli," the man says. "But we can't run around haphazardly in the middle of the day. Let's get to a clearing and regroup."

"But we'll have to start all over," the boy whines.

"Better than losing the trail completely."

I hold my breath as I hear them walk away and when they're out of earshot, I exhale. *That was close.* What could they be hunting in the middle of the day so close to the city?

A branch cracks behind me. *Oh no, they're back!* I turn around slowly, but instead of the boy and his father, I am face-to-face with the dark red eyes that stared me down in the restaurant. The beast hunches over as it watches me. It flexes its hands, revealing its long, sharp claws. Fresh blood drips from its chin, unless it's something else—but I doubt it.

"You need to go back," I whisper, unsure if I can move. "You don't belong in this world."

The beast tilts its head, listening to me. Does it understand what I'm saying? It shifts its weight, still watching me, then throws its head back and lets out a loud howl.

My entire body springs to action, and I start sprinting through the woods, as fast as I can, to get away from the beast. I can hear footsteps behind me and panic sets in.

"Help!" I scream, hoping someone is within earshot.

My feet hit the path that cuts through the woods, and a piece of me screams out with gratitude. I can't hear anything over the pounding of my feet hitting the gravel and the booming of my heart exploding in my ears.

The light from the break in the trees is up ahead, so close I can almost reach it. I falter for a moment, stumbling on a loose section of gravel, and I topple forward over my feet. I fall to my knees, and cry out in pain as the sharp gravel rips apart my skin.

I quickly look over my shoulder as I scramble to my feet. The wendigo is behind me, propelling forward as it grabs the trunks of trees and practically flies through the woods. A flash of white flies between us as the man jumps in front of the beast, holding his hands out. The boy is gone.

"Run!" the man says to me.

I scramble and start to limp down the path, but the howl of the monster screams out from behind me. I turn just in time to see the wendigo bring its long claws down against the man's shoulder and a flash of white breaks through the trees, blinding everything around me. I turn back to the path and run, and a loud roar follows me. The trees behind me rustle, forcing me to run through the pain, not stopping until I'm safe. I don't want to see what's coming.

Katya is standing behind the kitchen window, and she waves to me as I'm running. Her face quickly goes from happy to worried, and she disappears from the window, then reappears at the patio doors.

As she slides the doors open, I collapse into her arms, nearly knocking her over. My lungs burn from the run and my heart feels like it will explode from my chest. I lie there, unable to speak as Katya runs her hand over my hair.

"What is it, Daciana?" she asks. "What's wrong?"

But I can't answer her; I just stare out toward the woods, taking in the full severity of the monster that I let out last night. Tryan was right. The wendigo is nothing like the imp.

CHAPTER TWENTY-SEVEN

Katya cleans me up and gets me into bed. I still can barely talk as the wendigo haunts my thoughts. This is beyond anything I could have imagined.

"Now, Daciana." Katya sits on the edge of my bed. "You must take a breath and tell me what has happened."

I try to take a breath, but it catches in my throat. How do I explain what I've done? As my eyes meet hers, I know I don't have a choice. "There's something in the woods," I begin. "But that's not where it started."

I backtrack to my evening with Brennan, and explain what happened in the café. She flinches when I mention the alcohol, but her disapproval quickly changes to shock when I bring up the wendigo.

"How could you not tell me this?"

"Tryan and Liana said they were taking care of it. Plus, you were gone and I'm telling you now." She starts to talk again, but I cut her off. "Just wait, it gets worse. I just saw the wendigo in the woods."

Her mouth drops open. "Why were you out there when you knew this monster was on the loose?"

"I was following a boy and his dad."

"What?" Katya shakes her head. "You aren't making sense."

Ugh. I backtrack again to the day in the hospital when I saw the flash of white light. When I mention the father and son, she looks downright concerned.

"You're telling me you could see these lights?" she asks. Her eyes widen slightly at the edges. I nod. Katya looks away.

"I will call Tryan and Liana to check in on that man and his boy in the woods," she says, tucking me into bed. "There's no telling if they're still alive."

"I wish Constantine was here."

"Me too." Katya sighs. "But he had urgent business back home, and I did not want to take you away from your friends for your birthday party."

"Oh, my birthday." I groan, lying back on my pillows. "No one will come anyway."

"Then the two of us will party the night away." She smiles and leaves.

My mind is racing, but I manage to fall asleep. When I wake up, it's dark outside; I slip into the hall and see Katya asleep in her room.

I get a drink and slip back into my room. I notice I missed a call from Tryan, so I quickly call him back. The phone rings a few times before I hang up. It's after midnight; he might be sleeping.

My phone rings for half a second. It has to be Tryan. I dial him again.

"Yeah, what?" Liana's voice comes from the other end.

"Uh, can I talk to Tryan?"

"No."

"Let me talk to him."

"We're busy working."

"Obviously you have time to answer."

"You keep calling."

"Let me talk to Tryan!" My voice vibrates with my anger.

"Listen, Dacie." Liana's voice cuts with arrogance. "The big kids are too busy dealing with important stuff to talk right now. We're still in the woods, cleaning up another one of your messes, so I'm going to hang up now."

"Wait," I say. Then I hear Tryan's voice say, "*Who are you talking to?*" followed by a click, then silence.

My body fumes as I redial my phone. This time it goes straight to voicemail. *Argh!* I phone back three more times without leaving messages, before I throw my phone on my bed and lean back on my pillows with my head in my hands. *I hate Liana.*

Eventually, I fall back asleep. My dreams are filled with taunts from a hidden long-legged blond with no eyes, and a smirk on her face. I spend the entire time chasing after her as I try to wring her neck.

In the morning, I wake up in a panic. I've slept in and am going to be late yet again for school. I get dressed, throw my hair in a ponytail, and run downstairs. Katya is in the kitchen, calmly making breakfast and watching the news.

"What's the rush?" she asks.

"I'm late for school."

"No school for you today," she says, pointing her spatula at the television. "Too dangerous."

I turn my attention to the TV and watch a news report on a string of pet thefts in town. Fifteen cats and dogs all were stolen from their homes overnight.

"I'm pretty sure I'll be okay," I say. "Unless you're telling me I'm going to be mistaken for a poodle because of my bad hair today."

"Don't be daft," she says. "It's the wendigo. This is just the beginning. After yesterday, you are lucky you are alive. Two strikes, Daciana, you know what a third is."

"I'm out?"

"Exactly." She turns and serves me a plate with eggs and toast. "No more risks. You're staying in until that thing is caught."

"I highly doubt it will show its face in the middle of the day at high school." I poke my fork at my eggs.

"It has your scent now," she says. "It will seek you out."

I shudder at the thought of seeing those beady red eyes again. After I eat, I go up to my room and try to call Tryan again, but I still get his voicemail.

"Tryan," I say, finally leaving a message. "If you can't take one minute to call me back and let me know you're okay, well, then just don't bother to call me back at all."

I click my phone off and throw it on my bed, instantly regretting the message I just left. It wasn't Tryan who was being a jerk last night, it was Liana. But that doesn't excuse him for not calling me back.

Katya appears in my doorway and looks from the phone to me. Her forehead creases to match her frown, but I just look away. She can't cut me off completely from the outside world. That would be torture.

"Let's do some weapon training," she says.

"Really?" I jump off my bed in excitement. "Yes!"

I follow Katya to the training room, and she holds her hands in the air. "Which weapon do you want to learn about?"

I glance around the room. There are swords, like the one Constantine uses, and there's a mix of daggers, arrows, and different kinds of firearms. I reach out for a handgun and Katya eyes me carefully.

"Are you sure you are ready for a gun?"

I touch my fingers across the cold steel, but it feels foreign to me. I remember the men who killed my mother. They had a gun. I quickly recoil from the firearm, as if its touch burns my skin.

I spin around the room, looking carefully at all the weapons. My eyes settle on a small crossbow, hanging on the wall. It's not as daunting as the others that hang next to it, and it's less threatening to me than the firearms.

"This one." I take it down from the wall. It has a leather strap at its end, and a trigger on the bottom.

"Ah, yes," Katya says. "That was your grandmother's favorite. Now, bring it up to the den, you will first learn how to dismantle it and put it back together again."

"We aren't going to shoot it?" I ask.

"That's the easy part. First, you learn to respect the weapon, and then you can use it. You need to understand, Daciana, a summoner's strongest weapon is their paintbrush. We only use other alternatives in the direst of situations, and even then, we injure demons, we don't kill them."

"Why not?" I ask. "If something like the wendigo is so dangerous, why don't we just kill it and be done with it?"

"When a demon dies, another one is born to take its place," she says. "It is all about maintaining the balance."

"Fine," I say, "we kill the wendigo and a new demon comes. Big deal. At least the wendigo is gone."

"How do you think demons are born?" she asks.

"I suppose when bad people die," I say.

"No." Katya shakes her head. "Tortured souls become demons. All tortured souls were once innocent people, troubled, but still innocent. It's not their choice to become a demon."

"So if we kill a demon an innocent person dies to replace it?" I ask. "That sucks."

"Balance isn't always rational."

"I'll say." I hold up the crossbow and look through the scope.

Katya laughs. "That is not how you use it. This one is special. You strap it to your arm and pull the trigger with your hand. That way you always have it ready at your disposal."

I spend the afternoon learning about the crossbow: how to assemble it and disassemble, how to care for it, and how to wear it. Between every activity, I pull my phone from my pocket to see if Tryan has messaged me or called. Nothing.

Finally, I get to go back to the training room and practice shooting it. But shooting isn't as easy as Katya made it sound. After my sixth miss, I yell in frustration.

"What's going on with Tryan?" Katya asks, unexpectedly.

"Nothing," I say. It's not far from the truth.

"I see how frustrated you are all day, getting mad over little things," she says. "You keep looking at your phone, then get madder. Tell me, what's going on?"

"I don't have time for boys and their games."

"Ha!" Katya laughs. "It's usually the other way around."

"Yeah?" I ask, defensively. "He isn't the one stuck in a house, waiting for a phone call while I'm out running around with some guy."

"Is that what this is all about?" Katya asks. "Liana? Listen, you cannot run from your tovaros. Look at what happened to your mother."

"I'm so tired of people talking to me about my mother!" I yell.

Katya stares at me in surprise, and I'm suddenly upset at myself for my words. I know she didn't mean it, but Brennan's words at school still run through my head.

"I'm not my mother," I say in a quiet voice. I unstrap the crossbow and put it back in its place. Then I turn and leave the training room, heading upstairs to my bedroom.

I lie on my bed and check my phone again. No calls. Katya's right, I'm on edge because of Tryan. *Why won't he call me back?* I'm sick of sitting in this house doing nothing. I look out my bedroom window and make a plan. When it gets dark, I'm going to show everyone I'm not my mother.

CHAPTER
TWENTY-EIGHT

I call Tryan one last time and leave a voicemail, "If you want to see me then you can find me in the woods at midnight." There. See what happens when you don't call me back.

I hang up the phone, toss it on my bed, and go to my desk to start reading up on wendigoes. Unfortunately, there isn't a lot on the subject. Some notes say they don't like daylight, which would explain why the wendigo was hidden in the woods when I saw it last. Others say that they like to eat people. I shudder. So much for the domesticated animal theory. As for weaknesses, it doesn't give me anything more than to try to injure it from a distance to render it immobile before attempting to paint it back to the netherworld. I sigh and slam my book shut. It's only 11:30 p.m. and I still have half an hour before I meet Tryan. I can't wait that long.

I sneak out of my room, dressed in black to hide myself in the darkness, and slink down to where I left the crossbow. The training room lights up as soon as I step foot in it, illuminating the walls around me.

The crossbow hangs on the wall, where I left it after my outburst. I need to get over my mom issues at some point, but I'm just not ready yet. I grab some bolts and start to leave the room, but a glare from the gun rack grabs my attention.

I walk over to the gun rack, eyeing the weapons. Would it hurt to take one for backup? I reach inside, feeling the cold steel of a handgun, and recoil again. No, I'm not ready for that yet.

I sneak out of the house into the night, checking the clock in the kitchen before going outside. 11:45 p.m.—it won't be long until Tryan joins me. I duck as I run through the yard, passing into the shadows of the trees, to begin my hunting mission. *How hard can it be?* The wendigo is larger than the targets I practiced on and all I have to do is make sure I don't kill it.

The woods are quiet and my footsteps sound like thundering elephants as I walk down the path. I slow down and remember that this isn't a race. I need to take my time and focus like a summoner would.

Up ahead, I can hear voices trailing toward me from my right. I creep up behind a tree and crane my neck as far as I can to try to hear what's going on.

"Let's go back," Liana says. "We're supposed to be hunting the demon, not your stupid girlfriend."

Tryan's voice follows. "If you had let me talk to her we wouldn't be in this mess."

I duck low and take a few more steps into the woods, freezing when I snap a twig under my foot.

"Did you hear that?" Liana says.

"Dacie?" Tryan calls out.

"Shut up, you fool," Liana says. "There's a wendigo on the loose."

"We have to find her," Tryan says.

"Why do you always fall for the bad ones?" Liana asks.

Bad ones?

"I warned you to leave when you were with Caterina," she continues.

Caterina?

"Dacie isn't like Caterina," Tryan says. "You can't even compare the two. Caterina was experienced. Dacie is just young and doesn't know much yet. That's why I'm here—so she doesn't get hurt."

"Not like you to listen to orders." Liana laughs.

I turn back to the path, which is just a couple of feet behind me. Tryan's only here because he has to be—this wasn't his choice—it's an obligation. I was so stupid to think a summoner and tovaros could be more than fate. I look down at the crossbow in my hands and almost laugh aloud, what normal girl meets a date in the woods at night to hunt a demon?

When my foot hits the path, it touches something soft. I jump back and look down where I stepped. A dead rabbit lays there, splayed on all fours like an offering. I don't remember that being there when I came through a minute ago. I kick the carcass with my foot and it flops over, displaying fresh blood. *The wendigo!*

I instantly crouch into the defensive position Constantine taught me, and start scoping the area the best I can. It's hard to see anything in the dense woods in the daytime, let alone at night, but I force my eyes to focus as I hold up my crossbow.

The trees behind me rustle, and I spin around, shooting the crossbow into the darkness. Nothing. I continue to look around me, holding the crossbow out as it shakes in my hands. Another rustle followed by a twig snap. I turn again and this time when I shoot the crossbow, I hear something cry out and fall, and slowly make my way toward a whimpering sound from behind a nearby bush. I jump behind it, aiming my crossbow, only to find Liana.

"You shot me!" Liana says, holding her leg and staring at me like she's going to kill me.

I lower my crossbow. "You snuck up on me!" I'm less apologetic than I am defensive. "I thought you were the wendigo! Are you okay?"

"Help!" Tryan's voice yells, farther away in the woods.

"Go!" she says sternly.

I run past her, deeper into the woods, trying to follow the direction where Tryan's voice called. The further in I get, the denser it becomes. I end up stumbling over some fallen trees, tripping on a log, and losing my grip on the crossbow as I hit the ground. *Dammit.* I forgot to strap it on. I scramble around, grabbing at debris as I try to retrieve my weapon.

The bushes next to me start to rustle, and my head snaps toward them.

"Tryan?" My voice comes out slightly louder than a whisper.

A loud growl fills the air, and I scream and jump to my feet as the wendigo breaks through and howls at me. I turn and start running, but trip and hit the ground again.

The monster grabs me by the ankle, and I grasp at the dead leaves and sticks covering the ground around me. My hand lands on the crossbow, and I grab it tight and turn myself over, hitting the wendigo as hard as I can with the weapon. The wendigo lets go of me for just a second, which gives me enough time to load a bolt. As it turns back toward me, I aim and shoot—the wendigo recoils and lets out a howl.

I jump off the ground and run past the monster, hoping to lead it away from Liana and get myself closer to home. I get a few yards away before I hear the trees crashing behind me. I stop and turn, aiming my crossbow at the wendigo as it flies into the air toward me. I let off a shot just before everything goes black.

CHAPTER TWENTY-NINE

Slowly the word comes back into view, and I find myself racing through the treetops. My face stings from the whipping branches as I fly above the ground. Does the wendigo have me? I look around, but I'm alone—no sign of the demon anywhere. There's a loud bang, crashing against my eardrums. It's the sound of another heartbeat, beating out of rhythm from my own.

Suddenly I stop, gripping a branch, and peer below. The heartbeat is close. As I focus on the target, I can slow it down to the point where the swish of the blood pumping through the heart is audible.

Below, a person moves their hand through wavy dark hair. *It's Tryan!* I need to tell him I'm here, and I'm okay. I flex my fingers anxiously on the branch, feeling a hunger bite from inside my gut. I want Tryan; I'm hungry for him.

Pain shoots out from my chest. I rub my hand against it and feel something sharp. I glance down and see a bolt sticking out of my gut, with blood oozing out from the wound. *When did this happen?*

A voice calls out to Tryan from a few yards away. It's Liana. Thank goodness she's okay. As she limps over, her heartbeat gets louder and louder, and my hunger switches toward her.

Tryan gets up and moves toward Liana, and I see what he was guarding. It's me. My body lies limp on the ground of the woods below.

I shift on my branch. How can I be down there? What's going on? My hand goes back to the arrow in my gut again, and I look down. This time I'm staring at the sharp claws of the wendigo.

I scramble in the tree, and hear Tryan cry out. I look down and see he's spotted me, and is grabbing his weapon. *No!* I scream, but all I can hear is the howl of the wendigo. My body might lie on the ground beside Tryan, but my mind is trapped in this monster.

I turn away, flying amongst the treetops as I search out a sanctuary. I can hear other heartbeats, far off in the distance. I need to feed; my hunger is all-encompassing. *How far am I from Tryan now? Miles?* I break into a clearing, interrupting a campfire surrounded by people. Screams fill my ears as I grab on to the closest person. Finally, my hunger is satisfied as I feast.

My head slams against my skull as I try to refocus on my surroundings. *Where am I? Still in the forest?* I try to shift my arm, but the pain in my stomach is too sharp—*the arrow!* My panic increases as I recall my last memories of the campers, their faces frozen in fear.

I grab at my surroundings and feel bedsheets. I steady myself and focus my vision on the wall across from me. My thoughts come in so fast I can barely keep up with them as they swirl in my head like a whirlpool holding them under the surface.

"Daciana!" Katya cries out. "She's awake. Help, someone. She's awake!"

Katya runs from the room out into the hall, her cry for help echoing in the corridor. The white walls of the room come into focus and the beeps of machines surrounding my bed fill my ears. I quickly look down at my hands. *Thank God, all signs of the wendigo are gone.*

"No!" Katya's voice calls from the hallway. "You must stay. She needs you now more than ever."

Tryan's voice enters the room. It sounds gruff and tired. "I'll be back. She's this far at least."

"Tovaros," Katya says with an edge of warning.

"We have work to do," Liana's voice pipes in. "I'll bring him back later, I promise."

My head starts to spin, and I grasp at the bed railing. Tryan passes by my door, staring straight ahead as he leaves, followed by Liana, who looks into the room at me with concern. I must be dreaming if I think she's concerned about me.

Katya comes back to the room, but it's too late. As if my body can feel Tryan pulling further away from our tovaros-summoner bond, the energy starts to drain from my body and follow him. I collapse against my pillow, just as Katya reaches my bed.

"Daciana!"

"The campers," I manage to whisper. "I'm sorry. I couldn't stop myself."

In the darkness of my dreams, I'm back in the woods, cascading across the treetops, pulled toward the sounds of heartbeats all around me and driven by my hunger. But I know it's not safe to hunt in the woods tonight. Something is different—there's too much danger here even for me. My connection to this wendigo body is growing weak. Instead of feeling any bit of control, I'm nothing more than an observer stuck inside the monster's head.

I travel away from the woods to somewhere that's not aware of my kind. It's not long before I come across a lone farmyard with a single light flickering in the night, showing me a man walking across the yard with his dog. I take the dog first.

I wake up to the sunshine pouring through the blinds of my hospital room. I follow the rays as they trickle in, landing on my bed and jutting across my lap to the opposite wall, where Chantal is sitting. *This must be a terrible dream.* I push myself up, surprised and wondering if I'm still dreaming.

"You were crying out in your sleep," Chantal says, shifting uncomfortably in her chair.

"I don't cry." I push my words out through dry lips. "What do you want?"

"Here," Chantal says, jumping up and pouring me some water. The cool liquid dribbles down my lips as I try to gulp it back. A sharp stab rips across my ribs, and I cry out in pain.

"Man, you're in rough shape," she says, putting down my cup as I lean back on my pillow.

"Again, why are you here?" I ask, unable to hide the sarcasm in my voice.

"I—uh," Chantal begins, "well, it all seems trivial now that I see how rough you look, but, when I heard about your accident, I just had to come see you."

"So you'd have something else to gossip about?" I ask.

"I guess I deserve that," Chantal says. "Listen, I didn't come here to bug you; I just wanted to say thanks for telling Brennan I like him. I've been somewhat rude to you since you got here and, well, that was nice of you. Not the way you did it, but nice nonetheless."

"You're welcome."

"So, what happened to you? I heard you were attacked by a bear."

"I can't remember," I grumble. "I should probably get more rest."

"Yeah," Chantal says, grabbing her coat. "You're lucky, you know. Could have been way worse for you, not like those poor campers."

"Campers?" I say as she walks to the door. "Wait, what about the campers?"

"Oh," she says, "you didn't hear? Whatever attacked you the other night got a small group of campers. Apparently, they'll have to be identified by dental records."

"No," I whisper. "Do they know what it was?"

"A bear or cougar or something like that," she says. "Been a long time since one came so close to town. Like I said, you're lucky."

"Have they heard of anyone else?" I ask. Chantal looks back at me confused.

"No," she says, "I imagine it got scared away when Tryan and that girl found you. Doubt it'll do any more harm again before it's caught."

A nurse interrupts us, and checks on my IV. "It's time for you to go," she says to Chantal. "We have to keep this one sedated for a little longer."

"No, please," I say, and Chantal gives me a look of pity as she slips out the door. "I want to be awake; I need to be."

"Sorry, honey," she says. "Doctor's orders. You've got broken ribs and more. Just rest."

As the nurse leaves, I cover my face, wincing as pain shoots through my torso. Chantal is wrong; it's too late; the wendigo has already struck again. And every time I go to sleep I am going to be sucked into its nightmares. Black surrounds my eyes and closes out all the sunshine in the room.

I wake up in darkness; the skies outside my hospital window are overcast, hiding the stars behind them. I try to open my mouth to see if anyone is with me, but my tongue is so dry, I can barely swallow. I push myself up in bed and grab my glass of water.

"*Daciana,*" a voice calls from the corner of my room. My heart jumps in my chest, startling me, and I drop the glass of water on the floor.

A dark figure steps out from the corner of my room, shrouded in shadows that dance all around him. I try to call out for help, but my words catch in my throat, so instead I grab onto the side of my bed and try to escape.

"Who are you?" I ask, pushing the words out of my dry throat.

"*I am your past, present, and future,*" the dark figure says, stopping at the foot of my bed. A shiver runs up my spine, aching with every movement it makes.

"You were in the house the other night," I say, watching the shadows reach out from him and grab at the bed. "Why are you here?"

"The wendigo will bother you no more."

"What do you want?"

"*I want only one thing,*" the dark figure says, lifting its hand and pointing it at me. My heart begins to beat faster in my chest. As the figure extends his finger, a pain spreads from my abdomen up to my chest, and I cry out.

"Who is your summoner?" I ask through gritted teeth.

A flash of bright light interrupts us just as the dark figure opens his mouth. He screams in pain, then disappears in the blast, taking his shadows with him. In the doorway is the young blond boy, Eli, smiling ear to ear at me.

"You saved me," I say, panting as I lean back in my bed. Eli is still hanging out in the hallway as if he's afraid to come near me. "What was that?"

"A demon," he says proudly.

"What kind?" I ask.

Eli shrugs, looks around the inside of my room, and steps inside. "Father doesn't teach me about the demons yet. I just practice bending light. I'm getting pretty good, eh?"

"I'll say." I smile from my pillow. "I'll make sure to let your dad know when I see him next."

"Oh, no," Eli says. "You can't. I'm not allowed to talk to demon summoners."

"Really." I raise an eyebrow. "But you're allowed to hunt demons?"

"I'm technically not allowed to do either," he says, looking down at the floor, suddenly finding an interest in his shoelaces.

"Well, then, I owe you one."

"I better go," Eli says, looking out the door. "Don't worry. I'll keep an eye on you."

I smile to myself as he runs away. I'm exhausted from all my visitors today, or has it been longer than a day? The only person I want to see has yet to care enough to visit.

CHAPTER
THIRTY

True to the dark figure's word, my dreams are no longer haunted by the wendigo. But I'm sure he's not someone I want to be indebted. Aside from that, everything else is looking up. This morning my injuries feel less painful, and there are fewer machines beeping in my room.

Katya is asleep in the chair beside me, and I desperately want a drink of something other than water. I slip out of bed as quietly as I can, sliding down the sheets of my bed, and wince as my feet hit the ground. I'm determined to start moving again. It's time to get back to my life.

As I slip out into the hall, I go on a hunt for a vending machine. I smile to myself as I think of the word "hunt"; if Constantine could only see me now. Luckily, I don't have to go far to the vending machines. I return with my arms full of soda, chips, and chocolate.

I'm almost back to my room when Tryan and Liana come out of my door.

"What do you mean, you don't know where she is?" Tryan yells, throwing his hands into the air.

"Relax, Try," Liana says. "She was sleeping. I'm sure Dacie is fine."

"I'm perfectly fine," I say, approaching the group.

"Daciana," Katya says, running from the room looking frazzled. She throws her arms around me, and I wince in pain. "I thought something happened to you."

"Just an onslaught of hunger," I say, holding up my treats.

"I can't believe you," Tryan says. "Do you know how worried you make everyone?"

"I was gone for five minutes," I say, pushing past and entering my room.

"You don't care, do you?" Tryan says, following me inside.

I put my food down and spin around. Katya and Liana are still out in the hallway.

"I don't care?" I say. "Where have you been?"

"Busy looking for what did this to you," he says. His eyes are bloodshot, and his clothes are dirty. A flicker of regret crosses my mind.

"Don't worry about me then," I say quietly.

"Are you serious?" Tryan throws his hands up in the air again. I jump back in surprise. "There's no pleasing you, is there?"

"I didn't ask you to be here," I say, my temper rising. "Go back to whatever it was you were doing. You've been here once—and didn't even talk to me. Don't let me keep you from wherever you'd rather be."

"You're so … " Tryan begins. "You make me … " He twists his hands in the air. "Do you know how many people you've put in danger? How many lives you're responsible for? You have no idea what's going on out there! You're such a spoiled little girl."

"Tryan," Liana warns, but it's too late. His words cut through my anger like swords into my heart.

I narrow my eyes, and look straight into his. "I know more than you realize," I say through gritted teeth. "I didn't ask for this life. It's not my fault I was protected from it. Look how much good it did." I wave my arm around, then shrink back in pain.

A look of shock crosses Tryan's face as my nostrils flare. I'm not sure if he's sorry for what he just said or surprised he actually said it out loud. How long has he felt this way about me?

"There's no way you could ever be my tovaros," I snarl, turning away from them all. "We're a terrible match."

"Dacie," Tryan says, grabbing my shoulder.

"Don't touch me," I yell, then grab at my ribs again. "Get out of here and take *her* with you."

His hand lets go of me, and I step toward the window, gripping the sill to keep myself together. Everything's all mixed up, but I can't let it get to me. I am the reason the wendigo is out. I am a foolish girl. But I'm not going to sit here and cry about it.

A hand touches my shoulder again; I look up and see Katya.

There's no one behind her. Tryan and Liana are gone. I throw myself into her arms for comfort.

After I calm down, I lie back in bed and rest. Katya closes her eyes as she sits in her chair. But I can't relax. My mind races back to Tryan's words, and I play them over and over again in my head.

I change my thoughts to the wendigo in an attempt to forget Tryan for a moment. The last time I slept, I didn't dream about the monster. Weird. I figured I'd be plagued forever. I wonder how it happened in the first place.

"Katya?"

"Hmmm?"

"Have you ever been in a demon's mind?"

Her eyes pop open, and she watches me from her chair. "Yes. When I choose to be."

"How do you do it?"

"It's part of being a master summoner." She shifts in the chair, leaning toward me. "Dacie, tell me, have you ever entered a demon's mind?"

"After the wendigo attacked me, I started seeing it in my sleep. I think it's finally stopped."

"Hmmm." She nods, leaning back in her chair.

"Aren't you worried about me?"

"Not at all, my dear." She smiles. "From what I'm told you hurt it before it attacked you. I imagine that by taking that little bit of power from it, you were able to access some of its power."

I frown. "Will you teach me more about that?"

214

She pops one eye open. "Definitely not. That is for advanced summoners only. I'd keep that part of your abilities private, just between you and me. If it happens again, let me know. The longer you are away from the demon, the less it happens. It's like me and the ifrit; I keep him near so I can access his fire if I ever need to. Sometimes I see more than I'd like."

I lean back on my pillow. There is so much I still need to learn about summoning. Maybe one day I'll have to return to Romania to learn more.

After a short nap, Katya leaves for the house to get me a change of clothes. I spend the afternoon playing my conversation with Tryan over and over again in my mind. I'm so preoccupied that I don't notice Eli at my door.

"Ahem," he says, politely clearing his throat.

"Oh, hello," I say, smiling at his presence. "What brings you back? Are there any dark things lurking in the corners I need to know about?"

"No." He smiles shyly. "Just stopped to say 'hi.' Well, 'hi' and 'bye.'"

"Are you leaving?" I ask, letting a frown cross my face.

"No," he says, "but I think you want to." He shifts uncomfortably from foot to foot. I notice his boots look scuffed, like hand-me-downs.

"I wish." I roll my eyes. "Unfortunately I have this whole healing thing to deal with first."

"I can help," Eli says, a smile escaping the side of his mouth. He folds his hands in front of him and goes up on his tiptoes and back down again.

"You can?" I ask, raising an eyebrow. "Tell me more?"

Eli enters the room slowly, and in the light of day, I can see that he's skipping across the tiles on the floor, making sure not to step on any of the cracks, his blond hair bobbing with each step.

"I can bend light, remember?" he says as he approaches my bed.

"You mentioned that last night." I smile. "What does light do?"

"It gets rid of the darkness," he says. "It can heal; it spreads love and happiness and all that good stuff."

"You can do all that?"

"Not me." A blush crosses his pale cheeks. "The light. Just watch."

He spreads his hands out over the top of my stomach and closes his eyes, focusing intently. He starts to rub his hands together, then holds them out from his body toward the sunlight flickering in from the window. Slowly, he begins to point his hands downward, toward my body, and the light follows them, bouncing off his hands onto me.

A feeling of warmth fills my body, its intensity causing me to cry out. I break out in a sweat. The light fills the room for a few seconds before it disappears. I blink away the burned image from my retinas and find Eli beaming at me from the side of the bed.

"How do you feel?" he asks.

I sit up slowly; my aches are gone. I grab at my ribs, pressing my hand against them; the pain is gone. A smile slowly creeps across my face as I narrow my eyes at Eli.

"What are you?" I ask. "You're not a summoner?"

"No," he says. "Not the same as you, I mean."

"Are you an angel?"

A smile breaks across Eli's face as he starts to laugh.

"Eli!" a man's voice calls from the doorway. "What are you doing in here?"

Eli's eyes widen, and his mouth drops open. The man enters my room, not waiting for a reply. He grabs Eli by the arm, yanking him toward the door. Eli cries out in pain.

"Let him go," I yell.

"This is none of your business, summoner," the man says. "You should know better. Your kind isn't allowed around us."

"Wait," I say, jumping out of bed. My legs wobble as soon as my feet hit the floor. I stumble out into the hallway, chasing after the pair of them. "It's not his fault!"

Eli stares back at me, his face mixed with sadness and worry. The man pauses at a window down from my room, letting the afternoon sun fall over them. Then with a flash of light, the two of them are gone. I step back, grabbing the doorway of my room, in shock due to everything I just witnessed. *What kind of summoners can do that?*

CHAPTER
THIRTY-ONE

After a few more days of poking and prodding, Katya convinces everyone in the medical field that we have excellent family genes. The doctor releases me from the hospital in disbelief that I have fully healed in such a short time. I can tell even Katya is suspicious, but she doesn't speak a word about it, and I decide not to share my dealings with the other kind of summoners.

When we get home, I instantly run down to the training room. I have a renewed motivation: I am going to be the one to put the wendigo back. I know summoner law, and it's my only way to redemption. I need to keep moving forward; plus, the dark figure said it wouldn't bother me anymore. It's time to put an end to this.

Halfway through my drills, I notice Katya sitting on the stairs.

I'm not sure how long she's been watching me, but I don't care. I continue with my session and don't quit until I'm dripping with sweat, and my arms can barely hold another drill.

"Feel better?" Katya asks, handing me a towel.

I wipe my face and ignore her.

"Don't take your anger for Tryan out on me," she says.

"Ugh," I groan. "Tryan is the last person I want to think about."

"You can't avoid your tovaros forever."

I start to put away the weapons I trained with and wipe down my mats. Avoid Tryan? I plan never to see him again.

"Daciana—" my great-aunt begins again.

"Katya, listen," I turn, feeling my anger rising from the pit of my stomach. "I'm here training, so I can clean up my own mess. I'm going after the wendigo."

"You must be joking," Katya says, one of her penciled-in eyebrows rising on her face. "Leave that to Tryan and Liana."

"Enough!" I say, louder than I mean to. "I'm tired of Tryan and Liana. Why don't they go back to their old lives and leave me alone? They're perfectly suited for one another. I've never seen a better match."

Katya's voice cackles through the training room. I've never seen her so jovial about anything. "A match? Two tovaroses? Don't be silly; they can never be together."

I roll my eyes. It's even worse than I thought. "How romantically star-crossed," I say, slamming the crossbow back in its place.

"No." She chuckles. "You don't understand. Tryan will never look anywhere again; you and he are connected for life. Once a tovaros finds their summoner, they are never attracted to another."

"Tryan had a summoner once before."

Katya raises an eyebrow.

"Yes." I roll my eyes. "I heard Liana talking about Caterina. I assume that's his past you learned about. See, you don't know everything."

"I'm afraid there's much more to that story than what you *think* you know."

"I know if Tryan really was my tovaros he would have come to the hospital more than once."

Katya shakes her head at me. "Look at you. Your connection is stronger than any I've seen before. There is no other way you could have healed so quickly."

"This wasn't Tryan." I motion to my body. "You never told me I'd meet light-bending angel-people."

"Angels?" Katya says, her eyebrows snapped together, wrinkling her forehead. "What do you mean?"

"I'm sure you've heard of them," I say, passing by her and heading up the stairs into the den. "You know, bright beings. Like to play with light. Although I didn't notice any feathery wings."

"How long have you been cavorting with them?" Katya asks, following me. I ignore her and make my way to the kitchen.

"I asked you a question." Katya grabs me by the wrist and spins me around. She's stronger than I realized.

"I haven't been," I say, pushing her hand off mine. There's a fury behind her eyes that's making me uncomfortable.

"Tell me," she yells.

"No!"

Katya eyes me up and down, stopping at my torso and staring intently where my injury once was. She begins to shake her head and turns away from me, making her way to the front door. "I'll be back later. I have some things to look into."

I hear the gravel crunch under the tires of her car. What is it about the Brothers of the White Light that made her so angry? Right now, I need to focus. I pause at the doorway of Katya's studio, then pass by it on the way to my own. I'm in search of a willing subject to practice on, and I think it might be better if it was something I had full control over.

At my desk, I pull out my sketchbook and my charcoals. I'm not sure how this part of the job is carried out, but I know I've done it before. I pull out my summoner book and look up the lesser demon list. Water nymphs—that's what I want to try.

I start by drawing a scene that might appeal to water nymphs. My limited knowledge makes it a little tough, but in my mind I picture a serene pond, filled with lilies and other Monet-like scenery. When I'm finished, I lean back in my chair and admire my work. If I were a water nymph, I'd definitely want to hang out here.

I stare at the drawing, focusing on the lines and the shading, allowing the picture to take over my vision. Nothing happens. I try again, this time calling to a water nymph in my mind. Still, nothing. Frustrated, I stand up from my desk and walk over to the window.

What am I doing wrong? It was so easy every other time before. A splash interrupts my thoughts. I spin around and see the paper on my desk move slightly. I run over and see that something is trying to crawl out of the water. Even the paper around it is damp.

Quickly, I grab my charcoals and begin to draw a net around that section of the drawing just as a tiny face covered in gills comes out of the paper. Its eyes scan the room wildly as it flails against the net. A high-pitched squeal comes from its mouth as it falls back into the drawing and the water where it came from. The drawing sits peacefully on my desk. The dampness is gone, and not even the water shows signs of a ripple. I jump out of my chair and dance around the room. I did it!

I sit back down and take a deep breath. I need more practice. I pull out more paper and start flipping through the *Book of Summoning* until I get to Chapter Five. Here I make mental notes of some of the lesser demons and their preferred habitats, and start drawing.

The first drawing I attempt is a djinn, easily trapped inside any container. I choose a lantern, and laugh at the total cliché of it all, but there's something magical to bringing a childhood fairy tale to life. The experience doesn't come through as impressive, unfortunately. Instead of a large, turbaned spirit, black shadows start to fly up from the drawing. I quickly cap off the lantern, and everything settles back on the paper. I call it a win.

Next, I try a goblin. It's a little hefty of a demon to try out for a beginner, but I want a challenge. As I draw a mountain scene, where they apparently like to live, I start working on drawing one of the grotesque little creatures, but the image of the imp keeps coming into mind. The more I focus, the worse it gets, and before I know it, something is trying to crawl out.

I begin to sketch a house around it, to try to stop it from coming through. But before I can finish, the face of the imp pokes through. "What are you doing?" he squeals.

"Go back!"

"You're the one calling me."

I freeze. I didn't know I could do that. "It was an accident."

"I told you I don't want out. Just leave me alone."

The creature looks from side to side, checking out the corners of my room.

"What are you so afraid of?" I ask. "Is it the dark figure?"

"Shhh!" he says, panicked.

"So it is," I say, leaning closer. "What do you know about him?"

"I'm not telling you anything. Leave me alone."

"You better tell me, or I'll pull you through and let him have you."

"No!" he squeals. "Don't be so cruel. That wicked tovaros must be wearing off on you."

"I'm just learning more about how to be a summoner." I motion to the *Book of Summoning*.

His eyes grow wide at the sight of the goblin on the open pages. "Fine. I don't know much. I like to keep a low profile, you know. You can't get into much trouble when you just care about yourself. Anyways, whoever that dark figure is, he's looking for you. And he isn't going to let any demons get in his way."

"Why? What does he want?"

"That's all I know!" the imp yelps. "Now send me back!"

I hear the door downstairs close. "Daciana? Is everything okay?"

"You better not be lying," I warn. "I know how to find you now."

"Hmpf." He shoots me a dirty look as I finish the house, closing him back into the drawing.

So, the dark figure has put a warning out to all the demons to leave me alone. Hmmm. It sounds as if I'll have the advantage over the wendigo.

"Daciana?" Katya's worried voice comes from the other side of my bedroom door.

I scramble and cover up my drawings just as Katya opens the door. "Sorry," I call out. "Just deep in studying." I point to the open text.

She glances around the room and then nods. "Okay. I'm going to be working downstairs." She looks back at my pile of papers and raises an eyebrow. "Be good."

CHAPTER
THIRTY-TWO

I spend the rest of the day in my room, honing my skills at summoning and trapping demons in my drawings. After six successful attempts, I flip the pages to the wendigo and begin to plot out how I'll capture it. Everyone will see I don't need protecting after all.

Time passes until a knock interrupts my thoughts and I hear Tryan's voice float upstairs along with Katya's; they seem to be arguing about something. I step outside my door into the hallway and tiptoe toward the stairs to hear what they're talking about.

"We're close," he says. "We're going to need her help whether you like it or not, Katya."

"No way," Katya says. "It's too soon. Something's wrong; she doesn't trust you anymore."

"That's my fault?" Tryan says. "She's so damn stubborn, I don't know what to do with her."

"I'll go in her place," Katya says. "I refuse to send Daciana before she is ready."

"I'll call you when we need you," Tryan says. He comes into view at the bottom of the stairs; his wavy hair is disheveled, like when he was at the hospital. Hunting is taking its toll on him.

"Have you heard from Constantine?"

"Not yet," she says. "I fear the worst."

"Something is going on." Tryan shakes his head. "The Tovaros High Senate is keeping it all hush-hush, though."

"I fear light summoners are watching." Katya's voice is hushed to almost a whisper.

"That is never good," Tryan says. "I better go. Tell her I came by, please."

His eyes glance up the stairs, catching mine. I let out a small gasp and jump out of sight, pressing my back tight against the wall. His face looked like it was painful to see me. Before I can think of anything to say, I hear him leave.

Almost angry at myself, I return to my bedroom and close the door. I'm left with more questions than I had a moment ago and frustrated that I have no one to talk to about them.

"Nice room." I jump at the sound of Liana's sarcastic voice coming from my bed.

"What are you doing here?" I ask. "Or should I ask: How did you *get in* here?"

Liana motions to my bedroom window. "It was too easy; you should really do something about that."

"Why are you here?" I ask, throwing her my best dirty look and dropping into my desk chair.

"Listen," Liana says, leaning her elbows forward onto her knees, "you need to get over this problem you have with me and stop taking it out on Tryan."

My jaw feels like it dropped to the floor. My problem? "Maybe you're the one who should lay off Tryan," I say, narrowing my eyes.

"That's better," she says. "Nothing like a little jealousy to get the heart pumping. But seriously, you need to put these thoughts of Tryan and me out of your head. I'm taken."

"If Tryan really cared, he'd be the one in here." I cross my arms in front of me. "And you don't act like a girl who's taken."

"Oh, please." Liana rolls her eyes. "There's nothing between Tryan and me, and there will never be. I found my summoner long ago. Tryan is just a good, old friend. He's only interested in you."

"I'm not his first," I say, "who says I'll be his last?"

"So you know about Caterina?" Liana smirks. "You're not as naïve as I thought. Yes, she was someone he cared for deeply, but Caterina only cared about Caterina. Tryan thought he had found the 'one,' but I warned him that Caterina didn't truly love him. She was an older woman who used Tryan for his youth. She manipulated him to help her kill demons—that is not our job."

"Kill?"

"Yes," Liana says, sighing and leaning back against my pillows.

"Tryan paid a dear price when they were caught by the Senate. He has been on probation for the last three months, paying his penance. Since then it's difficult for Tryan to trust anyone."

"Where is Caterina?" I ask.

"Rotting in some summoner prison hellhole back in Romania," Liana says. "It's perfect really, poetic justice."

It must have been hard for Tryan, killing demons. He seems so disciplined, so guarded. How could he trust anyone again?

"Stop fighting yourself over all of this," Liana says, leaning toward me again. "Don't you see; you two are meant to be together. Tryan is just overprotective of you because of what he's been through."

"I guess."

"You guess." Liana laughs. "I will hunt you down myself if you hurt him." My anger shoots up into my cheeks. "Oh, don't look so offended. Come on, come with me. Let's get out of here and go find Tryan."

"I don't know."

"You don't want to stay stuck in this room any longer, do you?" she asks. "Maybe we'll even find the wendigo?"

I grab my sweater and toss my sketchbook and charcoals in my bag. Tryan may or may not want to see me, but I don't care. I'm going to get rid of this wendigo once and for all. Then maybe Liana will finally get lost, too.

CHAPTER
THIRTY-THREE

We take the long way around to Tryan's house, but no one's there when we arrive. Liana lets herself in as if she's lived there forever. We might have found a common ground, but we definitely didn't bond back at my house.

"So," I ask, lifting a bra off the chair before sitting down, "where do you sleep?"

"You're hilarious," Liana says as I toss her underwear onto the floor. "Honestly, if I wanted Tryan, I would have taken him years ago."

"Tell me about this summoner of yours then." I need something to wipe the thought of her and Tryan entwined together out of my mind.

A narrow smirk runs across Liana's cheeks and reaches her eyes. She leans forward on her knees and looks away, almost dream-like.

"His name is Nicolae," she says. "We grew up together; in fact, I've known him longer than Tryan. I always knew he had a crush on me, but I have to say, stringing him along was part of the fun." She stands and walks to the window, staring out at the woods across the street. The setting sun halos her lean figure. "All through high school he pined for me, then, when we turned seventeen, I gave in and committed."

"Why would you string along someone you liked?"

"Oh, Dacie." Liana smirks again, tossing her long, blond hair over her shoulder as she turns her face toward me. "You don't get it, do you? Once a tovaros and summoner have a connection and commit, there's no going back. You're together for life. It was the only time I could play a little with him."

"Why did you leave him then?" I ask. "Why risk his safety to come here and watch Tryan?"

"Tryan is a dear friend," Liana says, narrowing her eyes at me and looking away. "He's been in trouble ever since Caterina; Nicolae understands that. Plus, Nicolae's been working closely with the Senate. There are larger things out there, above even our pretty little heads."

"Where could Tryan be?" I ask, standing up and looking out the door. As if I had the ability to summon him, he appeared at the opening to the path in the woods. "Hey look, there he is—"

The treetops behind Tryan start to sway and tilt, moving closer and closer to him. He stops across the street as our eyes connect, lifting a hand as he waves to me.

"No!" Liana screams, running to the door and pushing me out of the way. I notice she's already carrying her bag. "Run, Tryan!" she screams, running across the lawn.

I watch in slow motion as Tryan ducks and turns toward the woods and Liana's long legs reach him in seconds. She grabs him by the back of the shirt, pulling him toward the house. Soon the two of them are running toward me before I've had a chance to move.

"Lock the door," Liana commands.

"Where's my knife?" Tryan asks. His eyes connect with mine and without a word I nod. Everything is good. I'm okay. We're okay. Let's do this.

I open my bag and pull out my charcoal and sketchbook. This is all I brought? What was I thinking? I feel underprepared to deal with any demon, let alone a wendigo.

"Just breathe," Tryan says, coming up to me. "And use this if you need to." He hands me a small hunting knife. "For emergencies only, deal?"

I let out my breath and my lungs release in pain. I must have been holding it in since I saw him across the street. Everything feels manageable again. "Deal."

"Good." He leans forward and pecks me on the lips. "Let's do this."

"Target is across the street," Liana says from the window. "It's out of the trees."

I look back through the door and see nothing but darkness between the trees. Then something shifts slightly in the shadows and suddenly those creepy red eyes are staring back at me like warning lights in the distance. Shadows spread around it, in and out between the surrounding trees. We seem to be attracting an audience.

"How are you going to get it over here?" I ask, turning toward Tryan. He and Liana look at one another, then back at me. "What?" I ask.

"Well, we need you," Tryan says. "That's been the problem all this time. The closest we've gotten to the wendigo is when you're around."

"What am I, bait?" I shoot a knowing look at Liana. "What would you have done if I didn't want to reconcile?"

She shrugs.

"This was a trap!" I say, staring back at her. Of course, Liana does what's best for Liana. She never cared about reuniting Tryan and me.

"Hold on," Tryan says. "It was my idea. I told Liana the other night—"

"You're not making me feel any better."

"Listen," Liana says, putting her hand on her hip and jutting the opposite one in Tryan's direction. "It's too late to argue. I know you want to help get rid of this thing; well, here's your chance."

I turn and look back out the window, watching the red slits that intently focus in my direction. I let out a sigh to release the stress that's pushing against my ribs.

"Okay, what do I have to do?"

"Just go out the door and stand outside," Liana says. "The wendigo will come to you and we'll attack it."

"But don't go too far," Tryan says. "Stay by the door."

"Okay," I say, raising shaky fingers to the doorknob. "Okay, I can do this." I look back over to Tryan and he nods, but there's no reassuring smile on his lips.

I clutch my sketchbook tight to my chest and force myself to step forward as I open the door. My eyes are glued to the woods across the street. Where's the wendigo? I can't see its eyes anymore.

I look back to the window and Liana shrugs. Tryan continues to stare across the street. I turn back, but nothing has changed. Even the shadows around the wendigo seem to have disappeared.

I let go of the door and take another step down the front sidewalk and stop. Still nothing. I jump as the metal of the screen door slams behind me, but it doesn't seem to rustle up any activity across the street. I take two more steps away from the house.

Then it happens. The leaves across the street begin to rustle as if a large gust of wind rushes through them, but it's not wind, it's hundreds of dark shadows flying out from the trees toward me. I scream and drop down to the ground, feeling their flurries fly above me, pulling at my hair as it whips about.

Their onslaught ends quickly, and I look up to see if there's more. But instead of seeing shadows, the red eyes are back and they're not in the woods anymore, they're attached to the rest of the wendigo, staring at me out in the open on the street.

I scramble up from the ground and run for the door. Tryan's standing on the other side trying to get out.

"Let me in!"

"I can't," he shouts. "Those shadows jammed it shut."

233

"Watch out!" Liana screams.

I turn slowly and see the wendigo on the lawn, watching me as its body heaves up and down as it breathes. Its smell of decay burns into my nostrils.

"Stay back," I shout at the monster, holding up my sketchbook. "You've broken the rules. You have to go home now."

The wendigo flexes its hands, revealing the sharp claws it attacked me with in the woods. I force myself not to run, and face down the demon I am responsible for.

"Don't move," I warn. "You were warned not to touch me." I step toward the demon, barely able to feel my legs as I move.

The wendigo throws up its hands and lets out a loud howl in my direction. I freeze, unable to run or protect myself. It jumps across the street, landing in front of me. I stare up at its matted fur, watching helpless as it raises a claw at me. I do the only thing that comes to mind—I pull out the blade Tryan gave me and stab the wendigo in the gut.

Blood squirts onto my hands and I jump back in shock. Did I really just do that? The wendigo screams again, but still brings its hand down at me. I cower, holding my arms above my head waiting for its attack.

At the same time, a loud smash comes from behind me and a bright light shoots past my face, hitting the wendigo in the chest. The monster stumbles backward and I jump to the side.

"Are you okay?" Tryan grabs me, pulling me away from the monster. "You're bleeding!"

"It's not mine, it's the wendigo's," I say, staring at my red hands. "What just happened?"

"Some help showed up," he says, pointing across the street. Eli and his dad are standing there, each holding a long string of light between them and the wendigo.

"Now's your chance," Tryan says. "Hurry up."

I run over to the wendigo with Tryan beside me. There it writhes on the ground, frozen by the light. Even the blood that was squirting from the blade sits petrified, as if it has already coagulated.

I fumble with my sketchbook, dropping it on the ground beside the demon. I fall to my knees and pull the book open to a sketch I had practiced on. This one was a scene of a large iron cell. I know exactly what I want to do.

I set the sketchbook on the ground next to the wendigo and start sketching the top half of the drawing. I'm nervous and my lines are crude, but I do my best to make it blend in with the rest of the sketch. I stare at the wendigo, suddenly unsure how to trap it in the drawing with my charcoals.

"Grab at its shadows," Tryan says. "Use them to draw it in."

I wrap my charcoals around the wisps of shadows emanating from the demon's head. It begins to scream and fights harder against its constraints, so I work faster. Soon the lines of the shadows attach themselves into the drawing and begin to pull at the wendigo. The demon begins to break apart as the shadows pull away from it, filling the cell in the drawing. As the last ounce of the demon disappears, a loud howl fills the air. I quickly sketch in a roof, and seal the cell shut. Silence fills the air.

I stand up, stepping back from my drawing. Did I really do it? The wendigo can't be seen in the picture, but the inside of the cell is now filled with black.

I look at Tryan and a smile breaks across his face. I laugh out loud and throw myself into his arms. Tryan spins me around in the air and when I land I remember who helped us.

"Eli!" I turn, but no one's there. Both he and the man are gone.

"Where did the angels go?" I ask Tryan.

"Those weren't angels." He says, wrapping his arms around me. "Those were light summoners. Thank goodness they came."

I tuck my chin against his shoulder, looking at the empty spot where Eli was just moments ago. It was good they were here, but how did they know? I guess I shouldn't start questioning things, when everything finally feels like it will be back to normal.

CHAPTER
THIRTY-FOUR

School isn't the same the next day. Liana stayed back at Tryan's, insisting that she deserves one day to sleep in before she flies home tomorrow. She was able to convince the Senate that Tryan has a handle on everything, his summoner-tovaros bond being official.

I'm glad for a day alone with Tryan, even if we are in a school full of people. But as History begins, I lose my brief excitement. The teacher's eyes light up as soon as he sees me at my desk.

"Miss Cantar, it's nice to see you've graced us with your presence."

I shrug, trying to sink in my chair as low as I can.

"Please, come to the front and let us know what you learned about your family."

My stomach feels like a pit of stress. "I'm sorry. I don't have my paper."

He frowns. "Well, would you like to save some of your marks by enlightening us on some of the things you do know, to prove that you've actually done some work?"

I begrudgingly skulk to the front of the class and face my fellow students. Out of twenty-five, only three or four are paying attention.

"Well, the Cantar family came over from Romania."

"What did they do there?" a nosy boy named Alexander asks without putting up his hand.

I furrow my eyebrows and look at the teacher, but he only shrugs.

"They were gypsies. So anyways, they came here and with four other families founded the town. The end."

"Oh, I'm sure you found out more," the teacher says.

"Well," I pause, seeing I've lost two of the four that were paying attention. Suddenly, I realize I'm proud of my family. These people should care. We risked our lives for them and more, all just to keep the balance.

"They were run out of town, suspected of witchcraft."

A few people look up from their desks. I continue.

"While they were away a large hurricane hit town, killing most of the residents. All of the other founding families were killed."

Over half the class is paying attention now.

"Do you think they cast a spell on the town?" a girl I don't recognize asks.

I shrug.

Another girl joins in. "Gypsies have powers, you know. I saw it in a movie once."

"They returned after the storm and helped the town to rebuild," I continue. "If it weren't for them, the town wouldn't be here."

"I wouldn't come back where I wasn't wanted," a boy says.

I smile. "I think they just wanted to keep the town and the people safe for the future."

"Yep, they must have been witches," another boy says.

The class breaks out into an argument.

"Okay, calm down," the teacher says. "This is a class about history, not the supernatural. Thank you, Dacie. Good researching."

I sit down and smile, proud of myself for speaking the truth. Well, mostly.

Once I get out of class for lunch, I'm brought back to reality. It feels like everyone is talking about me. People are whispering and I'm sure I saw a girl from my afternoon chemistry class pointing at me. I slide in across from Tryan with my lunch tray and poke my fork into my salad.

"Wow," Chantal pipes up behind me. She spins around with her tray in one hand and her other entwined with Brennan's. "You healed like superfast."

"Yeah, I guess."

"No, seriously," Chantal says. "You were all messed up when I saw you."

"Good genes." Tryan pipes up. Chantal looks at him as if she just realized he'd been sitting there all along.

"Hmpf." She shrugs. "Or magic."

I almost blow my drink out my nose. Seriously, you tell one little story.

"Where's your *girl*friend?" Brennan asks Tryan.

"Sleeping in," Tryan says, folding his fingers under his chin and letting a smile cross his face. "She flies home tomorrow, really misses her fiancé."

Brennan stares at Tryan, as if he has more to say, but Chantal pulls him away from the table. I look after them wishing things could be different. No matter how close normal seems to be, it always escapes my grasp.

"Let's get out of here," I say, putting down my fork.

"After school," Tryan says, and I resentfully pick up my fork. "We've missed enough school lately."

When the bell rings, I practically jump from my seat and weave through the crowd to get to my locker and dump my books. I run outside and find Tryan leaning against his pickup, waiting for me.

"Where to?" he asks. As soon as the words leave his mouth, I know where to go.

"Give me the keys. I'm driving."

When we pull up at the cemetery gates, Tryan raises an eyebrow. "This isn't the first place that popped in my head," he says.

I drag him out of the truck and through the gates. We walk together as I slowly lead him to the mausoleum. Shadows dance between the headstones, but I ignore them. Soon we are both standing in front of the large CANTAR sign.

"Is this where you take all the boys?" Tryan chuckles.

I punch him in the arm, then walk to the back where the hidden ladder is carved in the stone. I climb first, determined to show him something he's never seen and give us absolute privacy.

From the top of the mausoleum, the entire town sprawls out below us. It's not that the mausoleum is that tall, it's just the way the cemetery is placed on a hill next to the town. I sit next to the angel who guards my ancestors while Tryan sits on my other side.

"I wonder how many funerals this angel has witnessed." I bump into Tryan's shoulder as I cross my legs.

"That's kind of dark," Tryan says. "This whole place creeps me out."

"You chase after demons for a living, and you find a cemetery creepy?"

"You'd be surprised what sort of things skulk around these places."

"I think it's beautiful. Why do cemeteries have to be spooky or creepy or dark? It's where people's loved ones get to be forever. It's like, when you die, at least you won't be forgotten."

"Do you miss her?"

"Who?"

"Your mom. You never talk about her."

I shrug, but inside, my guts contract together. What am I supposed to say about her? Mom was barely around. Mom liked to drink more than she liked her own daughter. "She did her best." It's all I can manage.

"What about yours?" I change the subject.

"Well … " Tryan sighs. "My dad was a tovaros like me, and, as you can guess, my mom was a summoner."

"You're lucky you got to grow up with two parents."

"I was. When I was thirteen they died. Not demons or anything, a car accident." Tryan starts laughing. "All those demons they dealt with, some more terrible than others, and then it's a car accident that takes them in the end."

I sit next to Tryan in silence, listening to the muted traffic pass by on the highway. "Were they good parents?"

This time he shrugs. "I think so. At least they tried to be. It was hard to have parents that had demanding jobs, but I had a lot of family around, so I was kind of raised by everyone."

The only family I know is Katya, and I just met her this year. Do I have a lot of relatives back in Romania? "It must have been nice to have so many people who loved you."

Tryan grabs my hand and gives it a squeeze. I rest my head on his shoulder. "You have lots of people who love you here."

My guts tug again, but this time it's a tingle. Is he saying what I think he is? I open my mouth, unsure how to reply, when we're interrupted.

"What are you two kids doing up there?" a caretaker grumbles from below. My head jerks up, and I stare down at his old face, the skin pulled taut across his forehead and cheekbones, but wrinkled and drooping everywhere else. It's not the ghoul assigned to watch over my family, it's a new one.

"Friend of yours?" Tryan asks me.

"Friend of ours." Eli and the man step out from the side of the mausoleum. "I'd like a word with you, tovaros."

Tryan stands and helps me up. He climbs down the ladder and looks up at me with a warning glance. "Stay close."

As we round the front of the mausoleum, Eli stays back with me while Tryan and the man move out of earshot. The caretaker goes in the opposite direction fussing with weeds around the surrounding headstones.

I bump my shoulder into Eli's. "Thanks again for all your help, both in the hospital and yesterday."

"No problem." Eli beams at me, his white teeth flashing in his full smile.

"Are you okay?" I ask. "I was worried about you when your dad caught you talking to me. He seems kind of ... easily angered."

Eli's smile falls from his face, and he looks down at his feet. "That's not really my dad. He's my uncle. I just call him *Father*, because that's his title. My dad's gone—he was killed a long time ago."

"I'm sorry to hear that."

"Don't be. I was three; I don't remember him. My mom married his brother. He's not that bad, just protective. Our kind isn't supposed to like yours."

"Well, I like you," I say. His face lights up. "You know, I lost my mom. It sucks." I am unsure why I'm opening up to Eli. There's something in his innocence that makes me feel connected to him. "It was last year—she was killed by these guys who broke into our house."

"Whoa, that really sucks," Eli says, looking back up at me. His round eyes soften, and his small hand slips into mine. My body relaxes as he squeezes my hand.

"Hey, are you hitting on my girlfriend?" Tryan says, walking up to us.

"You better watch out." Eli crosses his arms.

"Eli," his uncle calls out. "It's time to leave."

Eli looks back at me. "Maybe we'll see each other again." He squeezes my hand one last time and runs after his uncle.

"What was that all about?" I ask, watching the pair of light summoners disappear in a flash of light.

"Senate stuff from back home," Tryan says. "How do you know them?"

"Eli helped me when I needed him," I say. "What do light summoners do?"

"You know how your kind summons demons," Tryan says. "Well, their kind protects humans from demons. Their main job is to perform funerals, so they can protect the dead before they're buried so they don't get possessed. Sometimes they'll step in if a demon is out of control."

"What do they do if a summoner can't get a demon to go back?"

"They kill it," Tryan says. "And sometimes they kill the summoner too. Trust me, there's a reason your kind does not want to mingle with light summoners. They are against everything demon summoners stand for."

"I'm locking up early tonight," the caretaker grumbles from

behind us. The one I know has returned.

Tryan spins around at the sound of the old man's voice and jumps in front of me. "What are you doing here, demon?"

"I have more right to be here than you." The caretaker's eyes cloud in a flurry of darkness.

"It's okay, Tryan," I say. He looks back at me in confusion.

"The Cantars put me here to watch over their dead," the caretaker says through gritted yellow teeth.

"She's a Cantar, and I'm with her." Tryan clenches his fists.

"Let's go." I pull at Tryan's sleeve. He reluctantly lets me pull him away, back toward the gates of the cemetery.

"That's right Cantar," the caretaker calls after me. "Keep the balance. But watch that one—I can smell the dead on him."

CHAPTER
THIRTY-FIVE

"That guy is bad news," Tryan says as we drive back to my house. "I can't believe your family would allow a demon to watch over them. What's his story?"

"I have no idea," I say. "I've only met him once before. It sounds like he's been here longer than the rest of us."

"I don't want you going back there. I don't trust him."

I remain silent the rest of the drive, unsettled with the idea that Tryan thinks he can tell me what I can or cannot do. I've taken care of myself since I can remember; I'm not going to start taking orders from anyone.

When we pull up at the front of the house, everything is dark. Katya must be out. I stay quiet as I close the door and walk onto the front porch.

"Don't be mad," Tryan says grabbing my hand and pulling me

back against his chest. He looks down into my face. "Demons aren't trustworthy," he says. "Just remember that."

I relax my body against his and Tryan leans down and kisses me. His lips are soft and gentle, and I melt against him. The stress of this last month melts away.

A shiver runs through my body and Tryan mistakes it for a chill. "Let's go inside," he says, pulling my hand toward the door.

As Tryan grabs the handle, the door creaks open. It's not locked? He looks back at me with a frown creased across his brow. I push past him into the house.

"Katya?" I call out into the darkness. Nothing. Lights flicker into the kitchen through the open patio doors on the other side of the house.

"Come on," Tryan says pulling me outside with a finger to his lips. "This way."

We slowly creep around the side of the house, following the flickering lights to the back yard. Between the tall fence and the wooden siding of the house, we're sitting ducks. We slow down as we reach the back corner and Tryan grabs my hand.

"Let me go first," he says. "Please. Trust me."

I nod and hold back as Tryan passes in front of me. He peers around the corner, then holds up a hand for me to stop as he disappears into the backyard.

I shuffle around the corner, but Tryan is nowhere to be seen. Lights are hanging along the fence to the back of the property, flickering on and off.

"Tryan?" I whisper. No answer. I look back. Where is he?

"Tryan?" I call out a little louder this time.

"Surprise!"

The backyard lights up, and people jump out from the corners of the yard, hidden in the shadows where I hadn't bothered to look. I've spent so much time avoiding the shadows that I don't pay them much attention anymore.

"Happy birthday," Katya says, giving me a motherly hug.

"But it's not my birthday until tomorrow."

Liana pipes up behind me. "Then this party better go until midnight." When did she get here?

"You knew about this?"

She smiles and walks away toward a table filled with multi-colored drinks topped off with tiny umbrellas. Katya can't do anything plain.

"You like?" Katya says, motioning to the backyard full of people. Most of these faces I recognize from the halls at school, but I don't know any of their names. I spot Brennan, Chantal, Sophie, and Zack at a table and Brennan waves. I wave back as Chantal grabs his arm and pulls it down to hers.

"I like," I say, smiling as I turn back to Katya. Where did Tryan sneak off to?

"Constantine said he'll be home soon," she says. "He didn't want to miss the party."

"Is everything all right then?" I ask, wishing I knew more about the goings-on in our homeland. "Is the Senate upset still?"

"For now everything is fine," Katya says. "It will all work out in the end. Always does. Anyways, don't worry about things overseas.

Enjoy your party. When it's over, I have a present in my studio."

"What kind of present?"

"A big, temperamental ifrit." She smiles. "I came across him the other day and thought he would be great training for you."

I shudder with excitement, remembering the first ifrit I saw, weeks ago before I knew anything about summoning or the fact that demons really did exist. Now I get to tackle one of my own. I wonder if I'll be able to summon his power like Katya can.

"Thank you," I say, taking Katya's hands. "Really. Thank you for everything."

"Go on," Katya says, the bottoms of her eyes filling with tears. "Go enjoy."

I make my way through the crowd, receiving tons of happy birthdays from my classmates. Some pull me onto the dance floor, where I let go and jump around with the rest of them. Others pull me aside into conversations about school, music, or what they're going to do after graduation. I don't even have a chance to feel awkward; everyone is treating me like I'm normal. It doesn't stop either, not even as the party dwindles down to a few stragglers.

Eventually, I break away and see the person I've been looking for all night: Tryan. He's leaning against a tree, looking away from the party, staring out into the dark woods.

"See anything interesting?" I ask, leaning against the other side of the tree. Our shoulders rub against one another under the pale moonlight.

"Now I do," he says, spinning around until he's facing me. The warmth of his body nudged up against mine sends something electric to the tips of my limbs. His breath glistens in the cool night air. "You looked like you enjoyed yourself tonight."

"You watched me?"

"I will always be watching you," he says.

I loop my fingers around the bottom of his shirt and tug him toward me. "I wish you would join me instead."

"I could be persuaded," he says, leaning in. His lips brush against mine and send a shiver down my back as he kisses me softly at the edges of my mouth.

"Are you cold?" he asks, pausing for a moment.

"Don't stop," I whisper.

"Look at you two lovebirds," Liana's says as she passes by. "It's time to wrap this party up. Happy seventeenth, Dacie. Sweet dreams." She winks as a smirk crosses her lips, then disappears into the woods.

"I have to go," Tryan says, leaning his forehead against mine. "Your aunt is waiting for you. It's almost midnight."

"I'm not going to turn into a pumpkin," I laugh. "Stay."

"No," he says, playing with a lock of my hair, "it's traditionally for summoners only. It's going to feel overwhelming tonight. All your shadows are going to finally become real."

I linger for a moment in Tryan's embrace. "Will it be scary?"

"No," he whispers. "Just remember, they need you. You'll be fine."

"I'll be inside when you're ready," Katya calls out.

"That's my cue," Tryan smiles, pecking me on the lips. "I'll see you tomorrow."

As he walks away, our hands stay entwined, stretching apart when he disappears into the shadows of the woods. "Good night, Dacie," he calls out. I watch until his shadow is gone.

I turn away and pick up some garbage strewn at the end of the lawn as a reminder of the party. As I clean up, I think about Tryan's kisses followed by his words. I hadn't thought about what would happen once I could see demons. Would they be everywhere? At least I have Katya to help me through it.

Something rustles on the path in the woods. I pause and look into the darkness and see a figure watching me. My heart skips a beat. Is it Tryan?

"What are you doing back here?" I ask, walking toward him. "I have to get inside soon."

The grandfather clock from the foyer chimes the midnight hour through the open patio doors, and I glance back at the house. When I look back to the woods, the figure steps out from the shadows of the trees into the moonlight.

My breath catches in my throat. It's not Tryan; it's the man from my dream. The figure—who has always been cloaked in darkness—is here, watching me.

"What do you want?" My voice comes out in a harsh whisper.

He moves toward me, shadows gathering all around him. His broad shoulders cast their shape on the ground in front of him, reaching out toward me.

"Daciana?" Katya calls from the house. "It's time!" I quickly glance over my shoulder, then look back. The figure has disappeared into the woods.

"Stop!" I yell, chasing after him into the darkness.

CHAPTER
THIRTY-SIX

Branches whip against my arms as I chase the dark figure off the path and into the trees. With every step I take, he gets closer and closer, and just when I think I can reach him with my fingers, he disappears into the darkness.

I stumble into a clearing where the moonlight breaks through the trees. Spinning around, I look for the man who haunts my dreams, but darkness surrounds me. The hair on my arms lifts and all my senses sharpen. It must be midnight. I'm officially seventeen.

"Show your face," I yell out into the night.

"Hello, summoner," a deep voice calls from behind me. I whirl around and see him hidden at the edge of the clearing.

"Come closer," I growl. "Show your face."

"Be careful what you wish for," he says, stepping out of the shadows.

"You do not have your tovaros or your weapons here to protect you."

He's right. I stare down at my hands, empty of all the tools I require to put this demon back to the other side. My fingers are shaking from the adrenaline of the chase.

I look back up at the man's face, hidden under a dark hood, and gasp at what lies beneath. His features are gone, replaced by nothing but a swirl of dark shadows that hold up the hood on his head. I thought I was supposed to be able to see demons now?

"What do you want from me?" My voice is barely audible.

He holds up his arm and strikes it down in front of me. An invisible force pushes against my head and chest, the pressure making me stumble backward.

"You are already protected by the tovaros's spell," the dark figure sneers. "He must be near."

The clearing fills with a burst of shadows, like the ones that followed the wendigo to Tryan's house. They spin around the edge of the clearing, swirling faster and faster as they grow in number, closing in the space between me and my freedom.

"I'm seventeen now," I say, trying to watch out for the shadows behind me.

"You are turning fast," he says. "My little ones can sense it."

"You can't hurt me. I'm a summoner."

"*I am Diavol,*" he says, rising in front of me. "Your mother couldn't protect you forever, and neither can your tovaros."

My heart falls against my chest. "What do you know about my mother?"

"The sounds of her last screams still echo in my ears like the sweetest sonata." He laughs. "She was all-consuming—so beautiful, so talented, and so torn apart by her doubt. I waited many years to find her—take her. She put up such a fight, I had no energy left to take you when I was finished. But she's not here to save you now."

"Damn you," I say, striking out at the dark figure. My arm brushes through him, and I scream out from the icy shards of pain that pierce my skin.

"Dacie!" Tryan's voice comes from outside the clearing.

"Your tovaros won't be around you forever." Diavol's voice rumbles in the air. "If you want answers about your mother, you will have to seek me out—alone."

The shadows around us begin to take form, each one more gruesome than the last. Their features slowly start to appear in the shadows: a sharp claw here, a menacing eye there. I can feel myself changing too as I become a summoner. My senses sharpen to the new smells and sounds forming all around me.

"Dacie!" Tryan is close. Very close. But he's not going to get here in time to stop Diavol.

"Wait," I cry out as I fall to my knees. "Tell me, how will I find you?"

"You must seek me out the darkest night of the year." Before I can ask anything more, the shadows flying around Diavol fly up into the night sky. As my powers transform, I catch a glimpse as Diavol's face just before he disappears with the others.

"Dacie," Tryan says, grabbing me just as my knees give out.

"He killed my mother," I stammer as I lie in Tryan's arms, staring after the monster. "It was Diavol."

Tryan helps me up and supports me as we find the path home again. I stumble among the brush, where once shadows danced but now small creatures crawl and scuttle away into wisps of shadows.

"How can you stand it?" I ask Tryan. "How can you see all of these terrible things everywhere and not go crazy?"

"You'll learn to control it," he says. "Don't worry, it gets better. Soon you'll be able to select which ones can contact you and which ones can't. You have the control, Dacie. You are the summoner. Remember they *need* you."

I don't want to be needed anymore. I don't want this family curse. It's what killed my mother, and it's what's out there, waiting for me. All hope has fallen. Now that I'm seventeen, I will never be able to feel normal.

As we round the last turn, a scream pierces the air followed by the smell of smoke. The woods open up into a large display of light and fire.

"No!" I cry out, letting go of Tryan. It's Katya.

The flames of my home light up the backyard. The entire house is engulfed in flames. No! Katya must have lost control of Ifrit. If only I hadn't run after Diavol, none of this would have happened.

"Katya!" I cry out, searching for any sign of her in the windows. I run around the yard looking for an entrance so I can save her.

The old wooden structure that made up my family home, which has stood here since the 1700s, begins to crackle and snap. I watch as my bedroom, where I learned to trap demons, collapses into the sitting room below. I shield my eyes against the burst of embers that flies into the night sky like an explosion of fireworks. Inside that room was my *Book of Summoning*, along with all the last mementos I had to remind me of my mother.

"Katya!" I scream as Tryan holds me back.

"There's nothing you can do," he says to me. I hate him for speaking the truth.

Shadows fill the skies as demons escape their painted prisons. How many did Katya have in her studio?—fifty?—one hundred? I fall to my knees. No one can stop this. Who will help us now?

Something moves from the side of the house and Tryan's grip on my shoulders tightens. I strain to see through the glare of the flames and make out Constantine's shape. He's dragging something. It's Katya! Tryan and I run over and help them get to safety.

"She's breathing," Constantine says, "but she's been badly injured."

"Katya," I cry out. She's moaning, but I can't tell whether she's conscious.

Sirens fill the air, but I know they won't make in time to contain the fire. The house is lost, and all that ties me to my past is gone with it.

Chapter
Thirty-Seven

"I am not ready to return to Romania quite yet." Katya's voice resonates in the hallway of the hospital. "I don't care what the Senate wants. When I have things ready here, we will return, and not a moment before then."

Constantine comes out of the hospital room, throwing his arms up in the air. "Your aunt is back to her old self," he says. "I'll be back in a bit."

I peer around the corner of the door, into the room where Katya has resided for the last two weeks. Her burns were severe, but luckily, after a number of skin grafts and the help of her tovaros-summoner bond, she has regained her health quickly. What can't be healed will become scars: both physical and mental.

"Daciana," Katya calls out in her thick accent. "Quit skulking in hallways and get in here and help me up."

I round the side of her bed and maneuver her into the wheelchair Constantine picked up for her. It houses the oxygen she's required to use every day for the rest of her life. Though I think that could be something that might heal over time.

"That foolish man thinks we need to sneak out and get back to Romania. I will not be run out of my home by some demon."

"There is no house anymore, remember?"

"I'm not a moron!" I recoil at Katya's tone.

She drops her head into her hand and shakes her head. "I'm sorry; I don't mean to take this out on you. It's just all this," she says, thumping her fist on her wheelchair. "I can't believe I have to live like this for a while."

"That's why Constantine wants to get you home," I say. "He thinks family doctors might be able to help you more."

"He forgets we're old." Katya laughs. "Our bodies aren't like they used to be. I fear this may be my penance for all the demons I let into this world over the last six decades."

"Don't be silly," I say. "You kept the balance."

"Sometimes I wonder about all we do," she says, staring out the large windows along the wall of her room. "Is it all worth it? Do any of them care?"

I stand next to her, watching the people walking along the sidewalk below. Do they know what truly happened in this town? If I told them about the wendigo, would they believe me, or lock me up?

"Of course they do," I whisper. "We don't want to live in a world full of demons running free, do we?"

She shakes her head.

"Hello, ladies," Tryan says from behind us.

I turn and smile at the large bouquet of flowers in his arms. Katya turns as well, revealing the right side of her face to me. The burns reach up past her hairline, and below the collar of her hospital gown. Her skin still looks raw and translucent; it will be a constant reminder of the fire unless specialists can figure out what to do.

"Tovaros," she says, opening her arms wide to Tryan. "You've brought the beauty of the outside to me." Tryan sets the flowers in Katya's lap after her embrace, and she sits silent, stroking the petals of the flowers.

"I passed by the house on my way here," Tryan says. "At least what's left of it. Did the Fire Marshall have any more information on what caused it?"

My body tenses at the memory of stumbling out of the forest and finding the house in flames—all those demons escaping into the night. I can't help but wonder if this was Diavol's doing.

"Nothing." She sighs. "Perhaps Constantine is right. Maybe it is time we leave this place of destruction and rebuild our lives back home."

"And never return to America?" I ask. The thought of going was exciting, but never coming back? It didn't sit well with me. I grew up here. My mother was here.

"Never say never." Katya waves a hand in my direction as she wheels herself to the bathroom.

Tryan joins me at the window. He stands behind me, so close I can feel his chest rise and fall with every breath. Right now, I want to get out of here and find somewhere safe to spend time with Tryan. But right now we don't have a home. "What are you looking at out there?" he asks.

"I'm looking at people." I sigh. "All the normal people who get to walk around and live their normal lives. They'll never know, will they? They'll never know what all of us sacrificed for them by going after the wendigo, or what Katya truly lost with that house."

"Normal." Tryan grunts. "Who decides that? Each one of their lives is different. Normal is in the eye of the beholder. When I get you back to Romania, you'll see what life is for people like us. I promise."

"Really?"

Could my life really be normal in a world of summoners? The same world my mother fled from, so she could raise me in America? If there was a chance, I wanted to see it. Maybe I could have a normal life after all.

But then I remember, I have a date with Diavol.

THE END

ACKNOWLEDGEMENTS

I have to thank Month9Books for loving *Summoner Rising*. They understood my vision, and found the perfect cover. I just adore it. Cheers to Georgia for falling in love with *Summoner Rising* as much as I did, and helping me to make it the best it can be.

I also have to send my thanks to Kahla, Bridget, and my mother, Faithe. These three make up my beta team, and I couldn't do what I love without them.

Since the day I signed with Month9Books, I have met a world of wonderful writers. Jennifer Bardsley and Elisa Dane, make up my direct circle of friends that I can bounce promo ideas off and get advice from. E.M. Fitch, Shaila Patel, and Jennifer M. Eaton are some new friends I've grown to appreciate. I will always love my #WOBooks team, especially Amy McNulty, Jessica Gunn, Pat Esden, Julia Ember, and Dorothy Dreyer. These five have become a part of my inner circle of bookish friends. As for booktubers, bloggers, and readers, I have to give a shout out to Shala (Shaegeeksout), Michelle (Bookaholic Banter), Hannah (aspiring author/avid reader), and bookstagrammer jennegan26. These four have become good friends, all because of their love for books. And I definitely cannot forget my new Instagram friend sharastar99 (whose insight into tarot cards and tea leaves was greatly needed).

For a girl who grew up in the middle of the Canadian prairies, this is beyond a dream come true. Thank you to my father and his made-up bedtime stories, and my mother who always pushed me to read.

All of you have helped to continue to make my dream come true. *Summoner Rising* is my second series, and a story I love deeply. When Dacie came alive on the page, I knew she was a heroine that needed to be heard.

MELANIE MCFARLANE

Whether it's uncovering the corruption of the future, or traveling to other worlds to save the universe, Melanie McFarlane jumps in with both hands on her keyboard. Though she can be found obsessing over zombies from time to time, Melanie focuses her powers on writing young adult stories to keep the rest of the world up reading all night.

Connect with Melanie: www.melaniemcfarlane.com

OTHER MONTH9BOOKS TITLES YOU MIGHT LIKE

THERE ONCE WERE STARS
OF THE TREES
PRAEFATIO

Find more books like this at http://www.Month9Books.com

Connect with Month9Books online:

Facebook: www.Facebook.com/Month9Books
Twitter: https://twitter.com/Month9Books
YouTube: www.youtube.com/user/Month9Books
Tumblr: http://month9books.tumblr.com/
Instagram: https://instagram.com/month9books

THERE ONCE
WERE *Stars*

She never questioned what she was
told until the impossible became real.

MELANIE McFARLANE

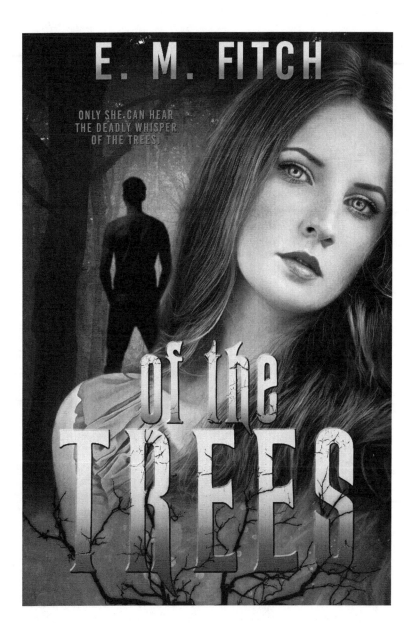

E. M. FITCH

ONLY SHE CAN HEAR
THE DEADLY WHISPER
OF THE TREES.

of the TREES

BOOK 1 IN THE PRAEFATIO SERIES

PRAEFATIO

A NOVEL

"This is teen fantasy at its most entertaining, most heartbreaking, most compelling. Highly recommended." -Jonathan Maberry, New York Times bestselling author of ROT & RUIN and FIRE & ASH

GEORGIA McBRIDE